One-Night Stand-In

One-Night Stand-In
Published by T Gephart

Copyright 2019 T Gephart
ISBN-13: 978-0-6483959-7-3

Discover other titles by T Gephart at Smashwords or on
Facebook, Twitter, Goodreads, or tgephart.com

Cover by Hang Le
Editing by Insight Editing Services
Formatting by Christine Borgford

One-Night Stand-In

T. GEPHART

Author's Note

This book was originally released as part of Kendall Ryan's Imperfect Love World in 2017. Since the rights have reverted back to me, all "Imperfect Love" world elements have been removed and the story has been expanded, but the core story has remained the same. This is the first time One-Night Stand-In has been offered to a wider audience and is a complete standalone.

1

Sarah~Then

IT WAS LATE.

Even though the room was pitch black, I had always had an innate sense of time, and it was definitely closer to noon than it was to morning.

I felt weirdly hungover despite barely touching any alcohol, a cloud of did-I-really-do-that making my body and brain foggier than anything I could have gotten from a bottle. No, this was from something *entirely* different, with the sweet ache in my muscles proof it hadn't been some weird vivid dream.

"Mmmmmm." His hand moved restlessly against my hip. His naked body nestled tight against mine while his impressive erection poked me not so discreetly. "How's my darling wife this morning?" His fingers slowly traveled up toward my breast, cupping it before he moved his lips to my neck. "Actually, don't tell me." He chuckled against my skin. "I like it better when you show me."

Shit.

What. Had. I. Done?

The question of course was rhetorical because, while the scenario was insanely out of character, there was no confusion as to what had transpired.

I'd gone to Vegas.

I'd met a ridiculously gorgeous man.

I'd "married" him.

I'd slept with him.

Sounds like every single Vegas story you've ever heard, right? Girl meets some good-looking guy at the bar and hauls ass to the Little White Chapel at three a.m. so drunk she can barely remember her own name. They say "I do" while a fat, satin-jumpsuit-wearing Elvis presides over the ceremony. Then they go back to their hotel room and have wild, unrestrained just-married sex until the hangover kicks in.

Except that wasn't what happened.

Well, the wild, unrestrained just-married sex happened, but that was another story.

My situation was different in that I had completely engineered it, and worst of all, didn't even have inebriation to blame.

Goddamn it, I was a dumbass.

No one plans a wedding in Vegas.

Well, certainly not smart people.

So when my boyfriend of two years suggested we hop a plane and get married in Vegas, I readily agreed on the condition we have a *planned* wedding. While I could accept getting hitched without sharing it with my friends and family, the idea of improvising a wedding made me want to dry heave.

Because I was a planner.

Call it a character flaw, a defect—whatever—but I didn't possess the ability to be impulsive. At least I thought I didn't.

And after three months of carefully coordinating our perfectly planned, non-spontaneous wedding, turns out my boyfriend/fiancé decided he didn't really want to be married after all.

He probably could have told me he had cold feet *before* I'd racked up thousands of dollars in credit card debt on non-refundable airline tickets and hotel accommodations. Would have really, *really* appreciated the heads up.

Instead, two days before we were scheduled to get on a plane and start our new adventure as husband and wife, he moved out of our shared Manhattan apartment and told me he wasn't *husband material.*

What! What? What kind of half-assed, lame excuse was that? We'd known each other for five years, dating for two and lived together for thirteen months. What did he think was going to happen?

I was too mad to even be hurt, furious I'd invested so much time in a man who clearly was terrified of formalizing a commitment. And maybe the fact I wasn't crying into my pillow was a huge wake-up call. That as much as I liked him, and believed we'd been wonderfully compatible—I wasn't in love with him.

Well, wasn't that a revelation, and had I not been the one to shell out all the money for the expensive lesson in self-discovery, I probably would have thanked him. Instead I was brainstorming ways to recover the cash.

Begging and pleading with vendors got me nowhere, with everyone giving me the same bullshit response. *No refunds.* So, rather than rampaging through the streets cursing his name, I instead did the first impulsive thing I've ever done.

Take the trip to Vegas myself and go through with the wedding without him.

Sure, I knew I wouldn't come out of it with a husband and the start of a new life. But I was damn well going to enjoy the hotel room at the Bellagio and the wedding cake. And while the dress hadn't been exactly traditional, it was white and stunning and deserved the chance to be worn. At least in the hope to attach some happy memories to it before I donated it to Goodwill.

And I would have totally been okay with sipping champagne in my wedding dress at the hotel bar by myself. No one needed to bear witness to my first failed attempt at matrimony. But it seemed fate decided that I wasn't supposed to be alone after all.

"Ummm." Yeah, oh wise one, words would be a good start. "Maybe we shouldn't, Kyle."

Or at least that's what he'd told me his name was. I couldn't be sure, much like I couldn't be sure having sex again this morning wasn't a good idea. I mean, damage had been done, right? Bad decisions had been made, what were another few more hours of being reckless?

"You don't sound convinced, Sarah." My new "husband" knew me so well; the soft kisses moving to my shoulder feeling just as delicious as they had last night. "I think we most *definitely* should."

Ugh. He was probably right.

Smart, intuitive and good-looking—no wonder I had found him so irresistible.

"That wasn't the deal." My body ignored my brain and my mouth as it twisted around to face him. "I only agreed to one night."

Wow, was he handsome.

Green eyes were framed by dark lashes, his face perfectly angular with a strong jaw covered in just the right amount of stubble. And lips that looked too pretty to belong to a man—pillowy and pink—spectacular for kissing.

And while I found it difficult to tear my eyes away from his face, the rest of him was pretty outstanding too. His tall muscular frame had been initially hidden by a tailored suit, but now there was no hiding how insanely toned and hot he was. Men with a body like that were featured on billboards. Usually in their underwear looking smoldering. Not in bed with ordinary girls like me. I wasn't even questioning the whys—surely he could have any girl he wanted—I was happy to live in ignorant bliss.

"What kind of man would I be if I left you here without at least giving you a morning orgasm? I very much like seeing my wife come."

Which he had, repeatedly.

The man had given me so many toe-curling orgasms last night, I wasn't sure where one ended and another began. It had never been like that, ever. I wasn't sure whether to celebrate or be sad that I would probably never come like that again.

"I'm not *really* your wife." It didn't need to be said and yet my mouth said it anyway. More to convince myself that this suspended state of reality would be crashing down at any moment.

"I *really* don't care." His lips moved to mine, his hands moving down my body with deliberate purpose. "I still want to make you come."

WOW.

Maybe I hadn't thought this whole leaving thing through.

See, a lot of things had transpired at the bar, hours before I said I do. I—serially responsible and rarely spontaneous—spilled my guts out to the handsome stranger who probably was just looking for a quick lay. I figured we'd never see each other again, what did it matter. Besides, nothing turns a man off faster than crazy talk about marriage. Of course, turns out that while talking to Kyle—we exchanged first names only—he didn't think my idea of going through with my wedding was so crazy after all. And then he decided he would be my stand-in husband. Perhaps it had been *him* who'd been crazy. Either that or he was going to extraordinary lengths for that one-night stand, I couldn't be sure which.

So, while it wasn't legal—no marriage license present or a witness in sight—we said words to each other that should have been reserved for that one true love. And while it had the capacity to sound tragic and even sad, it was really quite nice that our first kiss be after fat, satin-wearing Elvis pronounced us husband and wife.

It was a sweet first kiss. One that would have definitely gotten him a second date if our sham wedding counted as our first. But that sweet kiss morphed into something a lot less sweet and a hell of a lot more steamy. And damn if I didn't want to sleep with him. After all, it was my wedding night and we were in Vegas, surely this was the one time irresponsibility was acceptable, encouraged even. No one would even have to know.

So throwing caution to the wind—along with my inhibitions—I invited Kyle to my hotel room.

He did not disappoint.

If there was a prize for one-night stands, my fake husband was the jackpot. He was attentive, yet demanding. Aggressive, but knew when to back off. He didn't ask what I wanted, he just intuitively knew. Like he had read some secret ancient text that mapped out women's erogenous zones. He was the master of his domain and mine, and even though I knew this was a one-time deal, I couldn't stop myself from enjoying every last second.

"Waiiiiiiiiiitttt." It slipped out of my mouth, just as his hand slipped between my legs.

I was embarrassingly aroused, my body totally fine with whatever he had in mind. It was the other parts of me that were being uncooperative, mainly my brain that told me I should cut my losses and hightail it out of there before my dream guy hacked me into tiny pieces, or gave me a venereal disease. Thank God we'd used condoms.

"Tell me no, Sarah. Tell me you don't want this, and I'll get up and leave."

His hand in between my legs didn't move, staying eerily still as his piercing green eyes focused on mine.

I couldn't say it.

Couldn't tell him to stop because I didn't want him to.

I wanted this, him, everything that had happened in the beautiful, reckless twenty-four hours since we'd met.

"I won't say no." I whispered it, the words easing out of my mouth on a long and labored breath.

"Because you want to? Or because of something else?" He had amazing self-control, not moving a muscle even though I could see from the impressive bulge under the sheet he wanted to.

"Make me come, Kyle." I arched my back allowing my legs to open for him.

In another time and place I would never have behaved so shamelessly. But in the room, with him, miles away from my world and all my responsibility—I wanted it. I wanted to stop thinking so damn much and just experience it all.

"I will. I'm going to make you come so hard you won't be able to see straight." His lips spread into a grin. "Although, I pity your next husband. He's going to have a hell of an act to follow."

2

"SARAH, TAKE A SEAT."

Caleb Baldwin commanded a room whenever he was in it. The handsome Co-CEO of Baldwin & Blake had once been one of the biggest manwhores in all of Manhattan. But the woman sitting beside him had changed all of that, his wife and the other half of the powerhouse duo, Co-CEO, Adele Blake.

She was what I aspired to be. And while she was stunningly beautiful, it wasn't what you first noticed. Ambition. Power. Respect. She'd earned it honestly with hard work. Not because of her last name or whom she married, but in spite of it. It was something I wanted and was ready to fight for.

The two of them had managed to not only pull the company back from the brink of collapse and fight off corporate piranhas, but resurrected the firm to greatness. Baldwin & Blake was a force to be reckoned with, and one of the reasons I had been desperate to work there when I'd applied two years ago. I wanted the chance to not only be a part of something great but work with a team that was young, vibrant and hungry for success. It was the only part of my life where I could take off the restraints and leave *being a lady* at the door—the one place where I felt comfortable with the attention.

"You're both here." I nodded to Adele as I lowered myself into the chair. "If you're trying to let me down easy, you don't need to. I know there were a lot of applicants for the senior marketing role, but I can tell you there is no one who wants it more than I do."

Since returning from my faux wedding in Vegas, I had thrown myself into my work. Relationships were safely on the backburner as I focused on what was really important. My career and me.

While this hadn't been my first real job out of college, it was the one where I really cut my teeth. I knew they were looking for someone more *seasoned*, but what I lacked in experience I made up for in sheer determination. And if they were going to give me the thanks-but-we-went-with-someone-else speech, I wouldn't fall into a heap and cry in a corner.

"Relax, Sarah. No one is trying to *handle* you." The corners of Caleb's lips curved as he tried to stifle a grin. "You've more than proven yourself in the last few months, your contribution to the Brixton account was outstanding."

"But?" I said for him, anticipating. And I knew there was a *but* because if they were giving me the promotion, they would have said so already. And Adele was noticeably quiet; she would have been the first to congratulate me.

"Fine, you want it straight, we'll give it to you straight. You are one of the hardest working staff members we have. You accept each new project, and prove time and time again how capable you are, even against others who have more than double the time in the company. And when you negotiate, it brings a tear to my eye." He laughed, his face beaming like a proud father. "But you said it yourself, you don't have the experience to head up a team. And the last thing Adele or I want to do is set you up to fail. Which is why—"

"I wouldn't." Arguing was never a good strategy. It was too close to begging, but I couldn't stop myself. "You've based your decision on what I don't have rather than what I do."

"Let me finish." He shook his head, the smile not diminishing. "Which is why," he looked to Adele before retuning his eyes to me, "we want you to co-manage the position. We want to give you every opportunity to exceed our expectations, and we have no doubt you will. Which is why we think a partnership will work better. You are going to share the role with one of our senior executives from the Chicago office who is looking to make a move. Actually, the timing couldn't be more perfect."

"We'd share it? How would that work?"

Was this their subtle way of hand holding me or hooking me up with a babysitter? If they didn't think I was up to it, I would have preferred they just told me straight out.

"It means you are equals. He hasn't been with us long, but while he's fairly new to the company, he's got a good handle on the industry," Adele interjected, her voice reining in some of my agitation. Or maybe it was anger. I couldn't be sure which, and most of it was at myself because I obviously hadn't convinced them outright that I was capable. "Trust me, Sarah. It's a good thing and we think you'll work well together."

"He interned with Stockwell Media and was their golden boy for the last couple of years; some even say he was earmarked for partnership," Caleb continued, the information he was providing being committed to memory. In my head I'd already dubbed this guy my nemesis.

Good, I wanted all the information so I could wipe the floor with him later. "Keith Stockwell is still holding a grudge that he left." Caleb didn't even pretend that part didn't thrill him.

"But he doesn't know B&B like you do. He is good in a boardroom, but you are *better*. He can be a *little* impulsive, and while risks are part of the job, knowing when to back off is important too. And he doesn't have your attention to detail or your patience." Adele nodded, her smile sincere. "Not to mention your work ethic—"

"But it's not a competition. You'll be a team." Caleb again took over. "Each of you with your own strengths. Use each other to not only get the job done, but improve individually. In six months or so we'll review, see how it's working out. For all we know this move won't be permanent and he'll head back to Chicago."

"Six months?" It might as well have been six years.

I was being irrational, I knew I was. After all, they could have just given *him*—whoever he was—the job. He certainly *sounded* more qualified and he hadn't asked for this any more than I had. He would definitely hate it, he'd hate me too because if he thought I was going to be relegated to being his assistant or secretary, he was sorely mistaken.

"We thought you'd be pleased with your promotion. More responsibility, more pay, climbing the corporate ladder." Caleb interrupted my internal furor against my still-nameless adversary. *I will destroy him; he can go back to Chicago and leave New York to me.*

"Sorry, yes, of course. Thank you so much for this opportunity." My cheeks hurt as I forced the smile and tried to remove any trace of animosity from my voice. "You will not be disappointed for taking a chance on me." *And you'll both have front-row seats when I wipe the floor with this asshole.*

"Sarah, I know you might be a little disappointed, but working as part of a team is really important here." Adele looked at her husband, her eyes softening with what was possibly adoration. "We all have to work together, no one can manage by themselves. It's not a sign of weakness."

"Yep, team work." I maintained my smile. "I can do that."

I was lying through my teeth, but I couldn't very well tell them both I had plans to annihilate my soon-to-be co-worker. No, I had to bide my time, and then prove I could do it all on my own.

"Sarah?" Caleb eyed me cautiously, possibly because it wasn't the first time he'd called my name. I'd been too busy plotting to notice.

"Sorry." I shook my head—and hopefully my mood—as I lifted myself out of my seat. "I was just making some mental notes, things I can show him when he gets here. I want to make sure he feels welcome, made to feel part of the process even though we've already started."

"Well, that's really admirable of you." Adele smiled, her hand resting on Caleb's arm. "I knew we made the right decision."

"Thanks again." I straightened my skirt. "I'll get back to my desk and start working on our next proposal."

I didn't give them time to respond, shuffling out the door before my façade cracked and it became obvious I had no intention of being nice.

It was only when I was in the safety of the hall that I allowed my shoulders to slump in disappointment.

Damn it. Damn it. Damn it.

They could dress it up as an opportunity and a promotion, but to me, I felt the sting of rejection. And the office was supposed to be the one place I didn't feel that way.

My personal life—if you could call it one—was in the toilet. While I was glad I hadn't married my boyfriend/fiancé at that debacle of a wedding, I couldn't help but feel cheated out of the time I'd invested in him.

In us.

Time that could have been better spent elsewhere.

Maybe if I hadn't been so preoccupied with being part of a couple, I might have shown Caleb and Adele I was capable of doing this solo.

And this new guy they were bringing over from Chicago.

The one I'd been so enraged about I hadn't even asked his name.

I hated him.

I hated him and I hadn't even met him yet.

He could be a wonderful man. He could be considerate and hardworking, who knitted scarves for homeless people and I would *still* hate him. Nothing he could do or say would change that because he was the enemy.

"So did you get it?" Kennedy cornered me in the hall where I was still loitering, her face so full of expectation.

Kennedy was one of my closest friends and definitely the only person at work I felt comfortable talking to. She, like I, had assumed that my afternoon meeting with Caleb and Adele was me finally getting to sit at the grown-up table.

All morning we had carefully watched as the few other internal candidates marched out with slightly less bounce in their step than when they marched in. It was this line of thought that lead us both to believe they had either chosen me or I'd been beaten by someone from the outside.

"Kind of." I eyed the closed door I had recently walked out of, conscious that our voices might carry. "Let's go make a cup of coffee." I tipped my head toward the direction of the kitchenette hoping she'd take the hint.

"Kind of? What does that mean?" she whispered as we walked past co-workers, trying not to draw any unnecessary attention to us.

It wasn't until we'd made it into the kitchenette and I closed the door behind us that I let the fake smile drop.

"So, I have to share the position with some new guy from the Chicago office. We are going to co-manage. Together."

"A new guy? From Chicago? But why?" Cue the wide-eyed, open mouth I had probably displayed when I was told a few minutes earlier.

"Because I don't have the experience, and he does." I tried not to sound petulant even though I desperately wanted to stomp my foot. "Apparently we'll make a great *team*." The word tasted bitter in my mouth. "This is such bullshit." I didn't bother to continue fighting the urge, my stilettoed heel tapping on the linoleum as I paced. "*He* has no business trying to take what's mine."

"So what are you going to do?" Kennedy asked, her eyes narrowing cautiously.

"Ruin him and run him out of town." I half laughed, hearing the words out loud sounding more ridiculous than they had in my head. "I have no choice."

"Awesome, you know I'm going to want in on this." Kennedy straightened, her hands on her hips as she flashed a devious smirk.

"Kennedy, I couldn't ask that of you. This could go really bad, I mean what I am essentially saying is I plan to undermine and sabotage someone I'm supposed to be working with. Caleb and

Adele, they could fire me. I'm not going to have you risk your job for my vendetta."

"Pftt, you aren't asking, I'm offering. And you won't lose your job; they love you. If anyone leaves it will be the new guy. So, let's hear it. I want to know everything about him. The more we know about him the easier it will be to find a weakness. Give me his name and a few hours on the company server and I'll have a file compiled."

Kennedy had brought up a very valid point, the more we knew, the easier it would be, and at that point I knew almost nothing. Not even his name, which would have been helpful.

"I don't know. I was so riled up that I didn't ask. Not that it matters, we have two weeks before he gets here."

"Awesome. That gives us plenty of time. So, here's something that will cheer you up." She rubbed her hands together in villainous glee. "Your ex got arrested yesterday. Allegedly," she did the quotation marks in the air with her fingers, "he was involved in some insider trading scandal at Marks and Tyrell. He wasn't directly implicated but he knew. Which, as far as the SEC is concerned is collusion. You dodged a bullet with that one. Best thing you ever did was leave him."

Ok, so that wasn't entirely accurate. It was *him* who left *me* but I was in no mood to correct her. Not to mention it was literally two days before we were supposed to get married, which had prompted my trip to Vegas.

Of course I hadn't told Kennedy—or anyone else for that matter—that I went through with the wedding with some random guy I'd picked up in the hotel bar. No, that would sound tragic and pathetic, of which it was neither. Instead, I kept my stand-in husband/night of debauchery to myself and replaced it with an alternative version of events. Ones where I sat by the hotel pool and drank fruity cocktails and I didn't have hot sex with a man I'd just met.

"Maybe it's a sign that my luck is changing." I tried my best not to be pleased at my ex's misfortune. Not that I was sadistic and wanted him to suffer or anything, but if karma saw fit to punish him then who was I to argue.

"Sure is. And believe me, this whole new guy thing will end up the same way. It's your time, Sarah."

It sure as hell was.

"It's my time."

3

Sarah

IT WAS BUSINESS AS USUAL around the office as I glanced up from my desk. I had arrived early, determined to start on my secret pitch for Skyline Action Wear. They were a huge athletic apparel company that specialized in women's exercise wear. Not only did their apparel fit great, but also empowered women of all shapes and sizes to love their bodies, and not be scared to work up a sweat. Something I wasn't afraid of either. It was femininity with assertiveness, which is why I wanted them in the worst way. Not only because they were a huge fish—the biggest account any single team member had brought in—but because I identified with their brand. Women feeling good in their own skin who were not afraid to get dirty when it was required.

But working on the account wasn't my only reason for getting to the office before anyone else. I liked it when it was quiet, better able to think without the distractions. It was when I did my best work. Besides, I only had two weeks before the asshat from Chicago arrived, so I had to make each one of them count.

People had started to arrive around nine, grumbling under their breaths with oversized coffees in their hands as they walked to their offices, but it wasn't until almost ten that the buzz really picked up.

"Oh my God." Kennedy fanned herself as she sat down on the edge of my desk, her excitement level higher than usual. "The hottest guy I've ever seen just walked in for a meeting with Caleb. Sarah, I am talking out-of-this-world hot. God, I hope whatever business he is pedaling, Caleb closes him because I want a chance to work on that."

"Kennedy, you can't sleep with clients." It earned her a half smile because I knew she wasn't serious. Although, there was no harm in looking.

"You didn't see him. Trust me, this is worth breaking company rules for." She tugged at my arm. "Let's go take a stroll up on the executive floor so we can check him out when he leaves."

"Are you serious? We're not going to go check out some potential client like a piece of meat. Did you forget what I needed to do? I have bigger problems, like landing Skyline and proving we don't need the asshole from Chicago here."

While I could probably use the distraction, jumping into an elevator and loitering in the hallway on the executive floor in the hopes of seeing the "hot guy" didn't seem like a solid plan. I had an agenda, one that dictated I bring Skyline to Baldwin & Blake solo and prove what an asset I was.

One that didn't need a partner.

"Yeah, yeah. We can still do all of that. But if you don't come see this guy with me, I'm going to be very disappointed." She planted her hands on her hips, staring me down with a look that was supposed to be menacing. Pity, it fell just a little short of the mark.

I could have argued, but that would have taken longer. And

while I was decidedly sworn off men and all that went with them, Kennedy was still entitled to ogle and fantasize. Which was why I decided it was time to be a good friend, rolling my eyes and conceding it was easier to humor Kennedy and watch this poor guy leave. Then I could get back to important work uninterrupted.

"Fine, but don't say I don't do anything for you." I abandoned my laptop and rolled out from behind my desk.

Kennedy jumped up and down like an overexcited Jack Russell, happy she got her way as she followed me into the hall.

"So do you have a plan beyond just gawking at him?" I pressed the button for the executive floor as soon as we'd entered the elevator. "Might help if we have some reason for being up there."

"We need a file from HR." She lied with ease as the metal doors closed behind us. "You're looking to see there's no conflict of interest with the new client and our existing portfolios. Due diligence." Kennedy bit her lip to hide her smile.

"So you *did* give this some thought." I laughed as the elevator came to a stop, the doors opening on the upper floor. "Let's hope we aren't up here waiting too long considering I actually have work to do."

It seemed we weren't the only ones who had the same idea.

"Have you seen him?" Maggie from accounting leaned in, her hand discreetly hiding her shy smile. "He's gorgeous."

"I was downstairs when he walked in," Kennedy announced proudly. "He shook my hand and everything. He has really, *really* big hands." She laughed as Maggie joined her.

"You know what they say about the size of a man's hands." Crystal, from IT had slid in beside us, the audience growing with each passing minute.

Kennedy laughed as her brows rose. "He must have a really big—"

"Shit." She didn't get to finish, the curse flying out of my mouth as the door opened and revealed the mystery man, the one we'd all been dying to see.

Kennedy liked to exaggerate but it was one time where she'd undersold the truth. He was gorgeous. Tall, wearing a suit so impeccably cut it showcased an amazing body underneath. And while those muscles were kept hidden, his breathtaking face was on full display. The strong muscular jaw, perfectly formed lips and bedroom eyes, demanding the attention of everyone in the room.

His beautiful green eyes caught mine, those dark lashes widening as they took in the view. Or maybe it was because I not so discreetly swore. But deep down I knew he recognized me.

It was him.

There standing in the open doorway, next to Caleb was the man I had married in Vegas.

Kyle.

My stand-in husband.

I blinked, hoping it was maybe just a guy who looked remarkably like him, but fate wouldn't be so kind.

There was no denying it was *him*.

"Sarah." He smiled, the same perfect smile he'd worn when he'd met me in the bar. "How lovely to see you again."

He didn't seem fazed—cool, calm and collected, exactly how I remembered him. Only even more blindingly handsome than the memory. Me, I wasn't so calm, and if not for the stellar job by my skeletal system, I'd probably have been a puddle on the floor.

"You know each other?" Caleb looked between us, probably

surprised the man he had just had a meeting with was on a first-name basis with a member of his staff.

"Yes, we do," Kyle answered before I had a chance to say we didn't. "Although it's been a while since I've seen my *wife*."

Bam!

It was like the air had been knocked out of me, with the single word hitting me square in the chest. And I wasn't the only one who'd gasped, the choir of shocked hisses coming from all sides to disturb the silence.

"I'm sorry, what did you say?" Kennedy laughed, the first to react as she shook her head.

"He is joking," I threw in, adding a little laugh of my own. I sounded nervous and not at all convincing. "Kyle just has a crazy sense of humor."

"I don't remember you being so shy, darling." He laughed, not even attempting to let me off the hook.

"Ladies, is there something you needed?" Caleb gave Kennedy, Crystal and Maggie the get-back-to-work look that made them all scatter.

"Um, I'll grab that file from you," Crystal called after Maggie awkwardly, both of them powerwalking down the hall.

Kennedy hesitated for a minute, wanting to stay in what was either moral support for me or to find out more. I knew I was going to be grilled later regardless but after another pointed look from Caleb, she took a step back.

"I guess . . . I should . . .there's a thing." She pointed down the hall, shooting me a pained apologetic look as she too deserted me.

Great.

And then there were three.

"Not sure what's going on here but I don't like being in the dark." Caleb waited, looking to Kyle and then to me. "Either of you want to fill in the blanks." Though probably intended as a question, it wasn't.

"We met in Vegas, when I took some personal time a few months ago." I attempted something in the way of an explanation. "We barely know each other, really. We just, you know . . . Vegas." I really wasn't doing a good job of it.

"We pretended to be married, it's really not that big of a deal. It was for entertainment value." Kyle's voice had all the confidence I didn't have. "I just helped Sarah keep away unwanted advances. You know how it can be. Sometimes it's just easier having a man around."

Oh, I was going to kill him.

It was one thing to throw me off guard but it was a completely different ball game to insinuate I was a damsel in distress in front of my boss. That would not fly, not even by a long shot.

"Funny, I remember it differently." I smiled, trying to keep the venom out of my voice. "It wasn't me who needed any help. You just seemed so pitiful, drinking alone at the bar. I felt sorry for you and thought pretending to be your wife might help you save face. You know, with the ladies."

He threw back his head and let out a big guttural laugh. "That's cute. But we both know I don't need help in that department, sweetheart."

"Sounds to me like there are going to be some complications here." Caleb's jaw tightened, his smile not as bright as it was a minute ago. "And I don't like complications."

Caleb wasn't a man who liked surprises and I wasn't going to allow my poor judgment from a few months ago to reincarnate into my worst nightmare. Nope, whatever business they shared could be done without an issue and then Kyle could go ahead and move out of my life like he had the first time.

"Honestly, there is no problem. Not on my end, that's for sure." I smiled calmly, lying through my teeth. "Everything is just fine. We were just sharing a laugh, nothing untoward at all."

I hoped I wasn't overdoing the sickly sweet, or that either of them would see through my act.

"Exactly," Kyle responded, unwilling to let me have the last word. "Nothing at all complicated going on here. In fact, I have nothing but extreme respect for Sarah."

Damn him for trying to out nice me. Couldn't he have just smiled and agreed? Nooooooo he had to go in there and say how much he respected me.

I really did have such poor judgment when it came to men, especially when it came to husband material. He had seemed like such a nice guy in Vegas, and sure probably only acting that way because he wanted into my panties. But as it turned out he was just like the rest of them.

A mistake.

"That's great." Caleb's lips broke into a smile. "Might make the transition a little easier considering the amount of time you're going to be spending together. Meet your new partner in crime, Sarah, Kyle Drake." He slapped Kyle on the shoulder.

"What—"

The word wheezed out of me, thankfully leaving off the few curse words I was thinking, as I struggled with being able to breathe and talk at the same time.

No, this couldn't be happening.

Playing nice for a prescribed period of time was one thing, while whatever "business" they were doing was another. Working with him? Nope, that couldn't happen.

My brain scrambled to find something appropriate to say, but other than *fuck*, I was coming up empty. And while I was able to keep a handle on my freak out, my face was doing me no such favors.

"I thought you said there wasn't a problem?" Caleb looked at me skeptically, inviting me to announce my objections or to forever hold my peace. Ironic it wasn't the first time I'd been challenged in such a way when Kyle was involved. Fat, satin-wearing Elvis had a little more flare when he did it, and I didn't need to worry about losing my job.

My hands rose, immediately putting my boss at ease that there was zero problem even if I was lying through my teeth. "Oh, there isn't. I'm just surprised. It's all fine. Good. Great. It's excellent news."

Inside I was dying. Fighting the urge to run or scream. My worst nightmare had just become my reality.

Because it wasn't bad enough I had to "share" my new promotion, like a child in kindergarten sharing a new toy, but I had to do it with a guy who had seen me naked.

Shit.

How does that even happen?

It had to be a mistake.

A practical joke.

Something, *anything* where the truth would be revealed and I wouldn't have to work with him.

"I don't think I could be any more excited." Kyle's eyes actually gleamed, excited beyond measure, like he was enjoying the whole thing.

"This worked out great." Caleb smirked before taking a step back into his office. "Kyle, I'll email the rest of the paperwork later. Thanks for stopping by." He turned his gaze and shifted his attention toward me. "Sarah, show our newest team member the way out, will you. You can probably use the time to get reacquainted." He didn't wait for a response, leaving me alone with Kyle as Caleb closed his office door.

Without thinking I grabbed his arm and pushed him into the vacant meeting room, needing more than just a minute to compose myself before I *walked him out*.

"If you want private time with me, sweetheart, all you have to do is ask." He throatily laughed as the door closed behind us. "I'll be honest, the idea of you on this boardroom table—very very hot."

"Don't be ridiculous." I straighten my shirt, completely ignoring his suggestion. Sure, the memory of our night together was actually making my skin tingle, and other parts of me take notice, but that could have easily been my anger too. I was not aroused. That would be stupid. No man could just turn me on simply by being in the same room.

The heat lingered in the air, taunting me as I reminded myself to be angry. Still busy with my internal battle, it was he who spoke first.

"I thought you said you were a sales associate at Sephora?" An eyebrow rose as he leaned back against the table.

"You said you were a computer engineer at a pharmaceutical company," I shot back defensively.

Obviously we both had lied about our jobs. For me, it was a

matter of keeping it simple. Men got intimidated when they found out what I did. Besides, I had already word vomited way too much of my life story when I met him, keeping things like my full name and where I worked seemed like a smart decision. Clearly he'd felt the same way.

"Chicks dig nerds, I was trying it on." He smiled with zero remorse.

"You were *trying it on?*" I scoffed in disbelief, unable to see how he could be so cavalier about the whole thing. "What was I? A pair of freaking jeans?"

"Tsk, tsk. And you were so honest with what you did? You going to offer to wax my eyebrows for me?" He smirked, making him look even more handsome, if that was at all possible.

"Oh stop. You didn't care what I did." I deflected, not willing to admit I had been just as deceitful.

"Honestly, I didn't. You were a beautiful woman I was interested in sleeping with, your job was just a talking point," he answered with sobering honesty. "I was more interested in whether or not you screamed when I made you come." His eyes darkened and I had no doubt what he was thinking about.

"You are disgusting," I snapped, hating I had been so uninhibited with him. "I can't believe I allowed you—"

"To what? Allowed me. . ." He waved his hand waiting for me to continue. "Go on, finish the sentence. Because unless your memory is foggy, which is completely possible, it was *you* who invited *me* up to your room."

I hated that he was right. That I had wanted to sleep with him as much as he had wanted me. I hadn't been tricked into anything. While the pretense might have been slightly skewed, I was one hundred percent aware of the intention. I wanted to have sex with him, to lose myself in the random hook up, something I had never done before.

"Maybe I was drunk and had no idea what I was doing." I tried in vain to explain my motives. "If you were a gentleman you would have kissed me and then left."

"You had a glass of champagne and a wine with dinner, you were far from drunk. And you weren't looking for a gentleman, sweetheart. You were looking for a man, which is exactly what you got."

Gah! He was right. I got exactly what I had wanted that night.

I didn't want some sweet kiss goodnight. And didn't that just make me hate him even more.

"This is never going to work. You need to leave." I fought the urge to drop my eyes to the floor. I didn't want to look at him, for him to see how under my skin he was. But I refused to give into the urge. It wasn't just anger either. Part of me was still attracted to him, my body remembering exactly what he'd done to it. It was a cocktail of hot and cold and I couldn't decide which was worse.

Both then and now, the lust, the agitation. I wanted him not to matter at all, like I obviously didn't to him.

"Why the hell would I do that, I just got here." He shrugged with the same indifference he'd shown the entire time. "If you can't handle the situation, then maybe *you* should leave."

"But I was here first," I fired back childishly.

"Seriously? That's the best you've got." He laughed, taunting me more.

Man, I hated him.

Epic-level hate.

I hated his beautiful face, his sexy as hell body, and the way his lips tugged a little higher on the left side when he smirked. All of him.

"What are you even doing here?" I changed tactics, unable to continue to look at him as I shifted nervously on my feet. "The new appointment wasn't supposed to start for another two weeks."

"I don't start for another two weeks, but finding a place to live and relocating takes time, I was securing my apartment today." He kept his eyes on me and gave a perfectly logical explanation. "Unless you're offering your bed again. I'd be more than happy to play house with you, my darling wife."

I didn't even need to look at him to know he was smiling, enjoying this way more than he should.

"Stop it, you know it wasn't legal." I waved my hand dismissively, wondering why he had to keep bringing up our faux nuptials. "We were never *really* married."

"You weren't this moody when I first met you." He stopped suddenly, his eyes narrowing as he studied me closer. "Is it me? Or the situation?"

"I'm not moody," I snapped, irritated he could read me so easily. "I'm just surprised."

"Fine, then be surprised." He moved away from the table he'd been casually leaning against and took a step closer. "But we're going to have to work together, that isn't going to change. So whatever it is, *we* need to deal with it."

"Just tone down the asshole and things will be peachy." I forced myself to meet his eyes, my emotions all over the place. Why did he have to be so good looking? It would be easier to hate him if he wasn't. "And I wouldn't get too comfortable either, I don't see you fitting in around here."

"Oh really?" He laughed, holding his arms across his chest. "I have a fairly good idea where and how I *fit*."

Damn him.

I refused to look away, the heat traveling up my neck as I prayed I wasn't blushing. "Whatever," I huffed under my breath. "Oh, and you can find your own way out. It will be good practice for when you eventually leave."

Careful to keep measured, I turned on my heel and walked out of the meeting room.

My breathing was ragged, and I was beyond frazzled but I didn't look back. Instead I walked with purpose to the elevator and maintained my composure as I pressed the button to go back down to my floor.

Come on, move faster. I willed the elevator to hurry and put more distance between us. Even when it opened safely on my floor, I didn't dare stop. Instead I walked straight to my office, avoiding all eye contact until I was safely inside. It was only once my door was closed that I allowed my shoulders to slump against the wood and take a deep breath.

"Okay, Sarah." I startled at the voice of Kennedy sitting casually in my office chair. "Start talking, and don't even try and leave anything out."

It seemed my interrogation was going to come sooner than later. Oh well, maybe it was a good thing. Get it all out in the open so I had someone to talk to about it.

One thing was for sure, if I was going to survive working with him, I couldn't allow him to get under my skin like he just did. And I was still going to need to annihilate him. That part of my plan hadn't changed. Who knows, maybe it would be easier? My carnal knowledge might prove to be an asset.

Yes, this job was mine, and mine alone, and if I had to play dirty to do it then I wasn't above that.

"Get comfortable." I smiled, the tension in my body starting to ease slowly. "This is one hell of a story."

4

Kyle

I HADN'T PLANNED ON STAYING in New York.

Checking out my new apartment, picking up the keys and organizing the rest of the move from Chicago was what I'd intended to do. Now, all of a sudden, I had the urge to stick around.

No guess as to why.

She was beautiful.

Long blonde hair with brown eyes and a body too perfect to be hidden by clothes. It's what had attracted me to her in the bar at the Bellagio, all of it packaged together just waiting for me to unwrap. And she'd been even more exquisite when I got her naked.

Watching her come—well that was more fun than I'd had in years.

See, women weren't a problem for me. I could get laid anytime I wanted, and sure I was arrogant about it, but it was just that easy. I had a decent face, worked out and had a job. Throw in I knew what to do with my hands, mouth and dick and it made me the dude jackpot.

And that's all it took to *get* a girl. A well-placed smile and I had them eating out of the palm of my hand.

But it was *keeping* one that took effort, effort I had no interest in expending.

So yeah, when I offered to be her husband for the night I knew she was looking for no-strings sex. Plus, I figured I'd never do the marriage thing for real so why not role play a little. And I'll tell you something, just between you and me. It was kind of hot. Best part was, I got the fantasy without the fucking commitment.

Next day, she went her way and I went mine. And even though I would have loved to have spent a few more days with her, watching her writhe all over the sheets, that night would not be a regret.

But I won't lie. Seeing her again, knowing I would be working close with her, gave me a major hard-on. Which is why I was sitting in my new, unfurnished apartment on the floor rather than being back on a plane to Chicago.

I was moving, right? So best get the move happening sooner than later, especially since I had a shiny new incentive to stay in town.

"Keely." My younger sister answered the phone on the second ring. And yeah, our parents hadn't been super creative with names. Thankfully there were only two of us so we didn't end up sounding like the seven fucking dwarfs. "I'm sticking around a little longer. I'll organize the movers to box up the house."

"Kyle." I could hear the disappointment in her voice.

For months she'd been hoping the move was a knee-jerk reaction, that when it came to crunch time I wouldn't actually go. I'd been impulsive in the past so it wasn't out of character for me to do something rash, but this time it was different.

I was serious as a heart attack about leaving Chicago, even if the job hadn't panned out. I still would have left, found another firm to hire me even if I had to take a pay cut. And no amount of time was going to change shit.

"Don't start acting all dramatic." I laughed, knowing it would probably annoy her as I rubbed my hand down my face. "It's a short plane ride if you need anything. Besides, that new husband of yours will make sure shit is taken care of." I left out the part that he had already proven that in spades or I wouldn't have even considered leaving. "It's time."

"You don't have to go, Kyle. Just sell the house and move somewhere else. Get an apartment, get a dog. Hell, come live with me and Mike. Don't leave." I could hear the catch in her throat.

I hated when she did that.

She knew I couldn't stand to see her cry, and wouldn't you know, it was a talent she seemed to be able to perform on cue. Which is why I was glad this conversation was taking place over the phone.

"It's not just the house. I need a change. I need—" Fuck, who was even sure what I needed, but I knew I wasn't going to find it back there. "It's time, kiddo. I'll call the movers in the morning. And don't even think about ransacking my comic book collection. I've already boxed those babies up." *Along with almost everything else.*

Knowing I'd be moving soon, I'd been living out of a suitcase since I'd gotten back from Vegas. I couldn't bear living in the house like it was anymore, even though I knew the walls had nothing to do with what had happened inside of them.

"It was Dad's collection, and technically they should be half mine," she argued back.

"Sure, I'll trade you half Dad's comics when you give me half Mom's jewelry."

"It's *women's* jewelry, Kyle. You have no use for it."

"Oh you never know, I might get my ears pierced," I deadpanned. "Those Cartier diamonds would look awesome on me."

Keely laughed, her teary manipulation hopefully forgotten. "Or you could settle down, give them to your wife."

The idea of a significant other was something Keely brought up often. Not maliciously, but in her head she saw my future alone and miserable. She didn't see the parade of women that left my bedroom, which meant I was far from alone or miserable.

As for her plans, well, I had no use for them.

"I already have a wife, I told you. We got secretly married in Vegas when I was there last. Part of the reason why I have to stay in New York."

Funnily enough, my surprise nuptials had served for more than just one purpose. Other than the obvious outstanding sex I'd had with Sarah.

On returning to Chicago, after Keely had mentioned my lack of a girlfriend one too many times, I'd told her about the mystery woman I'd married on a whim. She'd assumed I was either joking or exaggerating, but it was enough for her to back off. The idea of me marrying someone without her rubber-stamping it was almost as bad as me not getting married at all. So I liked to pull that baby out of my back pocket from time to time. The fact it wasn't a complete lie made it just that tiny bit sweeter.

"Very funny." Her laughter stopped. "Fine, have it your way but I'm not going to suddenly forget I have a brother because you've moved. I'm going to call constantly. And visit when I can. And I expect you to come home every holiday." She issued her list of demands, her way of being okay with it all.

"I'll do my best, kiddo."

We said our goodbyes, me promising to call in the next few days and her promising to leave my comic books alone and no further mention of me with a woman.

So of course it made perfect sense when my thoughts turned to Sarah. Stupid reverse psychology at its finest.

It was a very welcome turn of events. And the more I thought about her, the more I wanted her—underneath me, begging for my cock.

Even though we'd somehow ended up working together—I wasn't even going to attempt to calculate the probability, but it had to be next to zero—there probably wasn't a good chance of sleeping with her again.

Not for lack of trying on my part.

Ha.

I couldn't think of anything more exciting than bunching that skirt she'd been wearing up around her waist and fucking her on my desk.

Or hers.

I was an equal opportunity fucker.

And the fact she was in my line of business didn't intimidate me, if anything it got me harder. But I could tell that for her it might be a deal breaker. So there was the challenge. Did I attempt to screw her, possibly ending up with a shitstorm at my new place of employment? Or did I keep my dick in my pants and pretend I don't know exactly the face she makes when I make her come.

Tough call.

Both options sucked so I was going to have to give it more thought. And I was going to need more intel. I picked up my discarded cell, dialed and waited.

"What do you want?" Her no-bullshit attitude always made me smile.

"I hear congrats are in order. What's it like to no longer have to work for a living?"

Camille Sawyer was a ballbuster. Smart, beautiful, and in an alternate reality I would have totally fucked her. One where she wasn't hitched to some multi-millionaire divorce lawyer and my sister wasn't married to her cousin.

Way too many complications.

She and I pretended to tolerate each other but we shared a mutual respect. And it had been her suggestion that I approach Baldwin & Blake. Not only had it been her old place of employment but also it was where her BFF, Adele, was CEO.

She hadn't gotten me the job that was for damn sure. Just like I didn't need help getting women, I didn't need help finding a place to work. But she definitely gave me the kick in the ass when my motivation had been lacking. Especially after . . . well, after it became impossible to continue to work for Stockwell.

I didn't even want to breathe the same air as those bastards, let alone be associated with them.

"You need something? Or do you just want to talk to someone who's more successful than you are," she bit back, always quick with a comeback.

"Ouch, Camille. You'd think married life would have mellowed you." I laughed, relieved she'd didn't give me the same guilt trip my sister had given me.

"Yeah, that's not going to happen, Marcus loves me just the way I am."

And while I didn't necessarily like the idea of matrimony, it worked for some people. My sister for one, Camille, was another.

"That's great, give him my regards." I meant that, just like Camille wasn't a bullshitter, I wasn't one either. But I could sense her waiting for the real reason behind my call and I figured I'd strung it out long enough.

"So, let's cut to the chase. Sarah Madison, what can you tell me?"

It only took a beat of silence before the warning came.

"Don't go there, Kyle." The light-hearted teasing was dropped as Camille turned serious. "She might look like a sweetheart but she's fierce. She could probably take you head on."

"Hmmm I bet she could." The thought alone got me hard.

I'd only seen a glimpse of that and I very much liked it.

"Don't sleep with her."

Yeah, a little late for that.

I rolled my eyes, not surprised she'd assume that was why I was asking. "This isn't about me sleeping with her." Not entirely anyway. "You know I want this to work, for me to stay at B&B. And I'm not leaving New York, so how about you give me some insider info and let me do the rest."

While I knew I brought value to the company, Baldwin & Blake were a loyal bunch. It wouldn't surprise me if I did something to upset one of them, they'd circle their wagons and send the intruder packing. And there was no guessing as to who that intruder was. Which meant I needed Sarah on my side, to be on board with this partnership because I wasn't going anywhere.

Besides, color me curious but I wanted to know more about the woman who kissed me sweetly and then sucked my dick like a champion. Not the kind of woman you turn your back on that was for sure.

"How do I know you're going to use it for good and not evil?" Camille was cautious, and rightly so.

There weren't too many men who wouldn't use information—especially if it was saucy or damning—as leverage. Maybe she was a communist in college or had a fetish for toe-sucking porn, all of which would go against the Baldwin & Blake ethos. But I wasn't looking to destroy anyone and I had an ace in my pocket that proved I could be trusted.

"You know I'll use it for good because Stockwell is still standing. And I took the highroad."

What I had on them was enough to bring them down to their knees. And I wasn't just talking financially but criminally as well. But, I'd given my word and it wasn't something I'd ever consider going back on.

"I start in two weeks, just get me what you can. I'm not asking you to dig through her underwear drawer," because if anyone was doing that, it would be me, "but get me some stuff to find me some common ground. I need to know what makes her tick. And I know you told Marcus what happened, but I'd appreciate if you kept it between us."

The less people knew about it, the better. Besides, there was only one place history needed to be and that was exactly where I planned to leave it.

In the past.

Especially since my future was already looking so promising.

"I've kept my mouth shut this long, haven't I?"

That she had and it was most appreciated.

"Thanks, Camille."

And I wasn't just thanking her for the information I knew she was getting me, but for what had come before it and the silence that would no doubt come after.

Trust was a big thing with me, and there weren't too many people who'd earned it. She was definitely one of the few.

"Yeah, whatever. But if this goes pear shaped, I don't want my name anywhere near it. I'm warning you, Kyle, do not fuck with her."

"Scout's honor." The smiled crept on my face.

"You were *never* a scout."

Well, that was true, my laugh coming soon after. "Stop riding me, I'll be good, I promise."

And while being bad sounded infinitely better, I was genuinely about not fucking *with her*. Now, if she asked me to *fuck her*, that would be a different story.

"Fine, I'll send you some stuff throughout the week. Bye."

"Bye." I bit back the grin as I ended the call.

It might be early days but I had a feeling I was going to really enjoy my time at Baldwin & Blake.

5

Sarah

I LOVED MORNINGS.

While other people battled, dragging themselves out of bed and getting their day started, it was when I was most productive. There were less distractions, less noise—time when I could think without having to compete with a phone call or something else. Which is why I was usually one of the first people in at Baldwin & Blake.

Unlike most mornings, I knew that today my quiet bliss had an expiration date.

I had been mentally preparing myself for Kyle's arrival. Approaching it with my usual business strategy, using the time between our heated re-acquaintance in the boardroom and his start date to collect information. I needed to learn as much as I could about my adversary.

Firstly, he was smart. After graduating from Loyola, he'd been offered an internship with Stockwell Media straight out of college. Which wasn't exactly news considering it was one of the few things Caleb had mentioned when first telling me about my partner. What he *hadn't* told me was that Kyle had been the only first-year intern responsible for bringing in a seven-figure account within his first three months at Stockwell.

He actively and aggressively sought business, and had a strike rate that hadn't been matched in years. No wonder he'd been their golden boy, and they were pissed at losing him. No amount of digging turned up his reason for leaving, but right before our Vegas trip, he inexplicably defected.

Could have been money—the most logical reason. But I was sure if given half a chance Stockwell would have matched, if not doubled, whatever he would have made anywhere else. Besides, assuming we were on the same salary, I already knew what he would be earning at Baldwin & Blake. It wasn't anything to scoff at, but it would be a while before he got offered a raise.

Not to mention he'd been on the fast-track to being a partner at Stockwell, so why go somewhere else? There had to be more to it. And I was going to find out.

So, apart from being gorgeous and having the ability to charm the pants off women—he'd certainly done that with me—I knew he was intelligent, business savvy and more than capable. Which meant I was going to have to work even harder to undermine him and prove he wasn't needed.

He had to have a weakness, something I could exploit. Something I could use to—

"Shit." I slammed headfirst into a wall of muscle. A chest it seemed, my head so deep in thought I hadn't been paying attention to where I was walking.

"Is this my welcome hug, sweetheart? I thought we were going to try and keep it professional."

Kyle.

My morning had already taken a turn for the worse and it wasn't even seven a.m.

"If that is how you hug, then keeping things professional is the least of your problems." I regained some composure and pulled my face away from his pectorals.

Never mind that he smelled delicious, a mix of dark roast coffee and masculine body wash. I needed to remember I hated him and sniffing him was not appropriate.

"And good morning to you too." He smiled and held up a large paper cup. "Black, one sugar. I heard you liked to get here early."

Firstly, he'd obviously been doing some research of his own. I wasn't sure if that was creepy—no comment considering I had been doing the same—or admirable. And secondly I couldn't believe he remembered how I took my coffee.

He'd ordered breakfast while I had been in the shower after our first and only night together and had asked how I wanted my coffee. We'd eaten and had more sex. And I thought for sure when I left, that I—along with how I took my coffee—had been forgotten.

If it had been anyone else, the gesture—him bringing me coffee—would have been incredibly considerate and sweet. But it was Kyle, which unnerved me.

I had no idea what his intentions were. For all I knew he could have put rat poison in it, and it was all part of an elaborate plan to kill me. Sure, a touch dramatic and possibly a little messy—he'd have a tough time disposing of my body before people arrived—but I wasn't ruling out anything.

I had made it abundantly clear that I hadn't wanted him working here and wanted him to leave. And if he were smart, he would be trying to get rid of me too, keep the promotion for himself.

"Thanks, but I've already had one," I lied, silently cursing myself for the loss of delicious caffeine goodness I most definitely could use.

"Well I guess more for me." He took a sip, his tongue sliding across his full lips as he lowered the cup. "Mmmm. So good." I was almost positive he was not talking about the coffee.

I ignored him and whatever innuendo he was throwing at me, choosing to walk away and head to the sanctity of my office. At least that had been my plan when I heard the heavy footsteps follow me in.

"What are you doing here?" I shucked my coat and bag, trying to keep the panic slash excitement—honestly, I wasn't sure which—out of my voice as he shut the door behind us. Being in such a close space with him was dangerous, it was easy to forget how bad an idea it was to kiss him. *No, he's the enemy, remember?*

"Didn't we already cover this? I work here." He looked bored, sinking into a chair without even asking. "You have a terrible memory. You should get that looked at." He took another sip of coffee, placing both of the cups on the desk.

I looked at them enviably, tempted to snatch one up even with my earlier objections. Lucky for me, his thinly veiled barb was enough to distract me.

"There is nothing wrong with my memory." Forcing the smile, I tried to forget what he looked like naked. "Yes, I get that you work here, but what are you doing *here* in my office?" And more importantly, when was he going to leave so I didn't lick the remnants of the coffee from his lips.

"Well, considering it's my first day, I thought we could strategize. A morning meeting so we could discuss business."

That was a completely logical notion, something that happened routinely especially when working as part of a team, and I was a little annoyed at myself for not thinking about it first.

"It's your first day, I thought you might want to ease into it. I didn't want to overburden you with details." *Good save, Sarah.* I leaned back in my chair, regretting not taking his offer of coffee. This conversation would be easier with caffeine.

"You're right, it's my first day but I don't want to waste it taking a tour to find the copy room." He leaned forward, his fingers drumming on my desk.

"Fine," I breathed out slowly, "let's have a meeting."

Kyle

There were two versions of Sarah.

One was the wild sex kitten who threw caution to the wind and had sex with a man she didn't know in Vegas. And the other was this buttoned-up powerhouse wearing the sexiest excuse of a skirt I'd ever seen. If her outfit was advertising she meant business, then baby I was buying. It wasn't just the look either, she knew what she was talking about. Her lips spewing facts and figures with ease, showing no intimidation when I asked questions.

I'd been given a brief about my co-manager before I'd left Chicago. Work history, strengths etc., I assumed she got a similar report of me. Of course, back then I hadn't connected that *Sarah Madison* was *Vegas Sarah*, why would I? And while her resume and listed abilities seemed impressive, I was more anxious to see what she could do. Coupled with the extra info Camille had provided, it was becoming obvious Sarah could more than hold her own.

Camille was right, Sarah was fierce, and I wasn't sure which version of her was hotter. I was also harder than I'd ever been in my life.

Lucky for me she stayed seated at her desk. Her beautiful eyes shifted between the computer screen and mine as she spoke so she didn't notice the present situation in my pants. Part of me wanted her to look down, to see the rod between my legs and ask me about it. Take it in that beautiful mouth of hers like she'd done at the Bellagio, and then let me come all over her perfect, firm tits.

"I think we should lead with a social media campaign. It's in line with their demographic." Her voice brought me to the present.

"Agreed, but you need a hook to make it go viral. Just throwing it out there online doesn't work anymore," I was able to choke out, which was difficult considering I was still thinking of her sucking my dick.

"True, we can talk to the social media team, see if they have any ideas." She grabbed a pen off her desk and made a notation in her notebook.

With her head lowered, the light coming through the window hit her face at the perfect angle. The sun spread across her skin showcasing her features as she wrote.

Fuck. She was beautiful.

I was really, *really* going to like working here.

"Am I going too fast for you?" She smiled, tucking a piece of hair behind her ear. Obviously there was a part of the conversation I'd missed. "I can slow down if you like."

She probably hadn't meant it to be sexual, but coming out of those perky pink lips, it sure sounded that way.

"I can keep up just fine," I assured her, resisting the urge to show her exactly how well I could *keep up*.

"Okay." She cleared her throat. "You should probably go to your office and work on what we already have." She shifted awkwardly in her chair, playing nervously with the earring in her right ear. "I have a meeting in an hour."

"Oh?" And *that* got my attention. She might be fierce, but she certainly had a tell.

I'd seen it before she'd propositioned me in Vegas. This cute little thing where she reached up and played with the lobe of her ear. And I didn't get where I was today solely on what I'd learned in a classroom in college. Nope, I had a knack for reading the room, came from having a grandpa who believed Texas Hold'em was an appropriate substitute for Go Fish. And it was that skill which had given me the edge over at Stockwell.

So, whatever or with whomever this meeting was with or for, she did not want me to know.

"Well if it's a client, shouldn't we be meeting them together?" I threw out a line, waiting for her to bite.

"I didn't say it was a client. It's just a meeting," she answered a little too quickly. "Nothing you need to be around for."

Yeah, right.

And I hadn't jacked off thinking about her in the shower that morning either.

Both of those statements full of shit.

"Okay then." I carefully rose out of the chair, doing my best to adjust myself as I stood. I wasn't trying to advertise that *someone* in my pants was very much interested but there wasn't a lot I could do about it either. "I'll leave you to it."

"Mm-hmm," she mumbled tight-lipped as her eyes floated down to my cock. And if her irises getting bigger were any indication, I was fairly sure she saw exactly what I had going on.

"We should reconvene later today." I pretended I wasn't packing a hard-on, giving her business as usual. "I'll let you get ready for your meeting."

And with a smile, I turned around, opened her office door and showed myself out.

It was probably an asshole move, walking out without saying goodbye, but I figured it was in both our interests. One, I didn't want to get hauled into HR over sexual harassment claims on my first day. Standing there, rocking wood while her eyes were on my crotch—was only inviting trouble. And two, if she was being evasive, she was playing dirty too. So keeping her guessing was totally in line. Fair was fair.

Besides, she wasn't going to tell me shit, that part was obvious. So heading back to my office seemed like the smarter option. Also gave me the opportunity to deflate what was in my pants.

Just a few doors down, my four walls were remarkably similar to hers. It was smaller than what I'd had in Chicago. The view was better, something I noted as I walked over to the huge pane of glass and checked out the skyline. Not that it mattered much; I had little interest in looking out of my window unless it was while I was fucking her against it.

"Hi."

There was a sharp knock at the doorframe of my still opened door.

"Um . . . I'm Kennedy." I turned around to the short brunette waving in my doorway. "It was open." She smiled, her chin tipping toward the door. "Just stopping by to say hello."

"Please, come in." I gestured to the chair in front of my desk.

Kennedy Elliot was one of Sarah's closest friends, which I knew thanks to Camille's report. So she was either in my office for reconnaissance, acting on behalf of Sarah, or her mission was unsanctioned. Both prospects pleased me more than they should.

"I know you probably have heaps to do, so I won't take up too much of your time." She quickly situated herself into the chair. "But you know," she gave me a wide smile. "Thought I'd be friendly."

Hmmm. Yeah. I'm sure *that's* what you were doing.

With no idea what her motives were, I found myself intrigued.

"Well, I'm new in town." I returned the smile, taking the chair behind my desk and giving her a little extra charm. "And it's nice to meet new people, especially friendly ones such as yourself."

"Oh, I'm sure lots of people are friendly to you." She giggled, biting her lip.

This particular type of exchange wasn't new. And typically, a girl like her—giggling and batting her eyelashes—would have her hand down my pants in twenty to thirty minutes flat. And that was being conservative. But that wasn't the plan today, which was ironic considering that's exactly what I'd wanted a few minutes ago.

It seemed my dick was feeling selective.

Interesting.

"So tell me, Kennedy, what do you guys do around here for fun? Any wild after-work drinks I need to clear my schedule for?" I pushed a little further, figured if we were going to flirt with each other I might as well use it to my advantage.

"No, nothing like that." She frowned, deflating slightly. "I mean, there's a bar not far from here we sometimes go to."

"Sounds promising." I leaned closer across my desk, looking her in the eyes. "*Sometimes* is one of my favorite times."

"Maybe we could get a group of us together, you know, to welcome you."

"I would like that." I didn't need to fake the smile. "A lot."

The air slowly passed through her lips on the exhale before she took another breath.

"Then it's settled. I'll organize everything." Her head bobbed as she slowly rose to her feet. "Just leave it to me." She backed slowly to the door.

"I can't wait."

6

"SO, DON'T BE MAD." KENNEDY burst into my office, her hands held up in mock surrender. "But I kind of offered to go to after-work drinks with your ex-husband."

"What?"

There were so many parts of the sentence that were cause for alarm. Funnily enough the *ex-husband* part wasn't the biggest. Which was a problem.

"He totally beguiled me. I completely understand how you married *that*. I mean I was in there for maybe a few minutes, and I would have stripped naked if he'd asked. I mean," she shook her head, screwing up her face in disgust, "I wouldn't because girl code and all of that. But ordinarily if you hadn't gone there, I totally would have."

"He's not my ex-husband."

"Fine, not *technically*." She eased into a seat. "But I would be totally claiming it if I were you. I would have found a way to make it legal too." She fanned herself, the animated smile on her face and goo-goo eyes a little too much, even for her.

"Kennedy, focus." I playfully shoved her arm, forcing her to sit up straight.

Kennedy was great. A ride-or-die friend who I adored, but she had a tendency to be scattered. Although even taking into account her usual MO, she was a little more scattered than usual. But then having spent time with Kyle, it wasn't hard to tell why.

Hell, he had *me* scattered this morning and I'd spent every waking minute trying to prepare for it.

And if I didn't know better, I would have been convinced he had been sporting an erection earlier.

Not that I'd intended to look. I had gone to strenuous efforts to make sure my eyes stayed a respectable height at all times and my mind did not think dirty thoughts. They may have wavered a little—my thoughts, not my eyes—but when he stood up, I had no choice.

Boom.

His crotch, right at my eye height.

And what I saw looked just as impressive as I remembered it.

Of course, I had to be imagining it because there was no way he'd been hard. That would be ridiculous, because we weren't doing anything remotely sexual. Unless spreadsheets were a kink I wasn't aware of. Sure *I* had been aroused. His sexy body inches away from mine and all the good times I knew it could deliver, which was even more ridiculous because that wasn't going to happen but . . . see—scattered! I was going to have to get a better handle on things.

Kennedy waved her hand in front of my face. "Earth to Sarah, now who needs to focus?" She laughed as she pulled me back to the present.

I shook my head, hoping thoughts of Kyle and what had or

hadn't been in his pants went with it. "Just tell me what happened."

"Okay, so I went in there to snoop." Kennedy settled in, getting herself comfortable for what was sure to be a story. "You know, see if he would spill any secrets we could then use against him." She lowered her voice, ducking her head slightly like perhaps the walls might betray her.

I sighed, rubbing my temples as I felt a headache coming on. "You shouldn't have done that, I told you, I don't want you implicated in which case we both end up fired."

As it was, what I was doing was risky. Besides not being completely honest with Adele and Caleb about how involved my relationship with Kyle had been, I was actively trying to undermine him. Not a good look, and something I was sure would get me my marching orders. The last thing I wanted was to be responsible for Kennedy losing her job, it was bad enough what I was doing was putting my own in jeopardy.

"Oh, please." She waved dismissively, her trademark confidence shining through. "I wasn't going to get caught. Give me more credit than that."

"So . . ." I urged her to continue. "You went in there . . ."

I sucked in a breath, more than just a little anxious to know what she'd found out.

"And he charmed me." She threw up her arms in disbelief. "Like he's magical or something. I'm not even sure how we got talking about drinks, but one minute I was looking to see if he had any open folders on his desk and the next I'm volunteering to organize a welcome party. Oh, by the way, you have to come. We're going tonight."

I wasn't sure what was worse, that Kennedy had fallen under

Kyle's spell—we already established through no fault of her own—or that I was now obligated to see him in a social situation.

"I can't tonight." I tried to think up a viable excuse, one that didn't sound like complete bullshit. "Kennedy, it's too soon."

My chest expanded before letting out a long breath. "Yes, he was only a one-night stand, but something was . . . I don't know, different. *I* was different with him. I was reckless, did things I usually wouldn't do, and now . . . look, I just can't."

I didn't want to admit that I didn't trust myself around him, buuuut, I didn't trust myself around him.

Sure, I could keep it professional when we were working, keep my focus on the tasks at hand. For one, I wasn't a mindless bag of hormones and secondly because I wasn't willing to throw away my career and a job I loved for any man. Maybe that's why it hadn't worked out for me in the past? My boyfriends not willing to accept that in order for me to be happy and fulfilled I needed the thrill I got in corporate.

Anyway, that wasn't important. What was important was if we took my commitment to being professional out of the equation, I wasn't sure what would happen.

Would it be like it had been in Vegas? Would I lose my nerve and tell him I was planning on destroying him? Would I throw myself at him shamelessly and beg for one more of those amazing orgasms?

Too many variables.

"I can't," I said as much for my benefit as for hers. "Go without me, I'll make up some excuse I had to work late or something."

She scoffed, rolling her eyes as her head tipped to the door he'd come through a few hours earlier. "Yeah, that won't work."

Damn it.

She was right.

He was already suspicious when I'd let slip about my Skyline meeting. If I made up some fictional work situation that he didn't know about, I would get a whole bunch of questions. It was only natural, especially given that we were *supposed* to be working together.

"Fine, I'll tell him I have a doctor's appointment." Not the best idea but one that would get me out of the pickle. "It means I'm unavailable for tonight and he can't tag along. Solves both the problems."

"Okay, but you might want to think of something else in case he asks questions." Kennedy didn't seem convinced.

"He won't ask, it's none of his business." People had doctor appointments all the time. Regular ones. It was part of being a responsible adult.

She winced, looking at me with pained skepticism.

"All right then, your funeral."

I had managed to get through most of the day relatively unscathed. Kyle had stayed in his office working on the projects we'd discussed that morning and I had been able to have my phone meeting with Skyline without drawing any unnecessary attention.

I was getting closer with them, I just knew it.

The few times we were in the same room, the sexual tension was definitely there. Like a weird, thick cloud that hung in the room, tempting me with his heavenly exotic scent—I was positive he purchased his cologne on the black market—and seductive bedroom eyes. But I didn't crack, not even once.

And I was almost positive it wasn't one sided. His eyes took more than a professional interest in the front of my blouse, the lick of his lips when I bent forward pleasing me more than it should.

Kennedy had been acutely accurate when she said he had some weird aura or something. No fewer than five women had turned their heads in totally captivation in the afternoon staff meeting so I couldn't be sure I wasn't under a spell and was imagining the whole thing.

Which is why I was keeping our contact to a minimum.

And my plan worked until it didn't.

"You ready to go?" Kyle walked into my office and moved over to where I'd tossed my coat and bag earlier this morning. "Kennedy is throwing me a welcome party." He smirked like he knew I had already been informed.

"Ah, yeah. She mentioned." I was careful not to fidget and look him in the eye. "I can't make it. I have a doctor's appointment."

"It's almost six, what doctor's appointment do you have? You don't look sick." He stood beside my desk, my coat and bag still in his hand.

Damn him.

His scrutiny was not something I wanted or needed, especially since it brought him closer.

"Well, that's personal and none of your business," I fired back confidently. I had been ready for it, forewarned that it might not be the best of excuses.

"Psychiatrist, huh? That's cool." A reassuring hand gently touched my shoulder. "You could have just said. I'm glad actually, Sarah. I applaud you keeping your mental health in check. Maybe mention the moodiness. Do you need a ride?"

"I do not need a ride and I am not seeing a psychiatrist." I shooed his hand and his sympathy away.

What the hell?

Why would he think I needed to see a shrink?

I should have just told him I had a date. Even if it was cliché it probably would have been easier.

"So, if you aren't sick or in therapy, it would be safe to assume this doctor's appointment is either a routine visit—which can easily be rescheduled—or you're avoiding me like you have been most of the day."

Why the hell was he so smooth and perceptive? Reading me like yesterday's news even though I was doing my best to keep my guard up.

Oblivious was what I wanted. In fact, the more ignorant the better. Instead, this guy had every angle covered. No wonder they'd been so desperate to hire him. If he was half as good at reading clients as he was at reading me, he'd double my numbers in six months.

Which would not do.

I hesitated, schooling my face not to reveal anything while I tried to decide how I was going to proceed.

Either way, it was a trap.

I wasn't sure I could convincingly sell that I wasn't avoiding him. Which, in turn, would make me look weak—something I wouldn't have. Alternatively, going out and spending a night drinking with him and an audience wasn't happening for all the reasons I'd listed with Kennedy.

Damn it.

"I can see you overanalyzing it, Sarah," he said suddenly, breaking through my internal debate. "It's one drink, what's the worst that can happen."

I already knew what the worst thing was.

I didn't do vulnerability, and I didn't want to make any more stupid mistakes. And the one time I'd let down my guard, and pretended that something I did wouldn't have consequences, it came right back to bite me in the ass.

"Fine, one drink. But it will be non-alcoholic."

I could do this.

Correction, I was going to do this.

Because I refused to be a quitter.

7

Kyle

I WAS AN INCREDIBLE NEGOTIATOR.

My parents had told me when I was younger I'd been born with the skill. Able to convince them that my bedtime shouldn't be set in stone, and that one last cookie wouldn't spoil my appetite.

What could I say? I was often indulged and I wouldn't make apologies for it. That, and I usually didn't need to beg a woman to have a drink with me. So my ego didn't want to let it go either. Especially not when I'd been thinking about her all day.

Not all of those thoughts were of her planted on her knees in front of me either. I'd given some serious consideration to the actual situation.

I had no more inclination to be partnered up in business than she did. It alluded that I wasn't capable of getting the job done myself. Which, of course, like any man, pissed me off.

So I could see where she felt slighted.

But unlike her, I knew all of it was temporary. One of us would retain the position with the other going on to greener pastures. Unless one or both of us fucked up royally, no one was getting fired and no one was getting demoted. So there was no point getting emotional about it.

My wife—I admit I got a strange thrill out of calling her that, especially since it aggravated the hell out of her—didn't share my clarity.

So, in the time she'd spent concocting a bullshit story about having plans meant that everyone who was meeting us for drinks had already left.

Big mistake on her part.

Meant she didn't have the buffer she seemed to desperately crave. And maybe I was an asshole, but secretly I loved I had her all to myself.

Of course I'd have preferred climbing into my car and taking her back to my place. Or hers, whichever. But I was going to have to satisfy myself by walking beside her as we made our way to the bar.

She took even and sure steps, matching my stride with no hesitation as we walked to The Waiting Room. Which was conveniently—for her, I'd have preferred it to be at least a block, even two, further away—located across the street.

The Waiting Room was a kind of place where the bartenders wore white shirts and you ordered single malt eighteen-year-old scotch. And it was exactly the sort of place I pictured her in. All buttoned up, predictable and safe, ordering something like a Gin and Tonic, or if she was feeling naughty, a dirty martini.

And I did like her naughty.

"Heeeeyyyy." Kennedy was the first to greet us, her eyes wide with surprise when she saw the two of us walk in together. "I thought you had that *thing*?" The latter part of the conversation reserved for Sarah.

"I rescheduled." Her smile not at all confident. "I thought it would be rude not to be here for Kyle's welcome drinks."

It was a mystery how those words didn't get stuck in her throat, and the thought made me smile. She was really trying, and to everyone else, she might have been convincing. But I knew better, knew it wasn't the danger of being rude that had her in attendance but some weird game of chicken we had going on. She wasn't willing to submit, and damn if that didn't give me more of a thrill than it should have.

My smile was easy, spreading across my lips with genuine amusement.

"Exactly, it wouldn't be the same without my partner-in-crime." My shoulder bumped playfully into hers. "I insisted."

Those beautiful brown eyes of hers shot me a heated look so fast I almost laughed out loud, the tight smile against her face threatened to crack her cheeks.

"Well, glad you were able to reschedule, Sarah," Kennedy fumbled, eyeing us cautiously. "Ummm, I'm sitting over there." She tipped her head to a round top, her purse being babysat by Joanna from accounts.

Rather than torture her further, I figured it would be more interesting to do what she didn't expect. So instead I kept her guessing, excusing myself and heading to the bar where, you guessed it, I ordered a single malt.

The place wasn't full, but I had to hand it to Kennedy, she knew how to pull a crowd on short notice. So it was of little surprise to see fellow B&B associates milling around the bar.

"So, Chicago, huh?" Peter, a guy I'd met earlier, took a mouthful of beer. "What brings you to New York?"

I'd gotten it a lot.

And my explanation differed depending if it was a man or a woman asking.

If a man asked—case in point—I'd give them the, "I wanted to play in the majors, and figured I'd have a better chance here."

That was bullshit of course, but it served my purpose. Just throw in a well-placed sports analogy and it usually got a grunt of approval. Which was exactly how Peter responded.

"Well, you definitely came to the right place." He nodded enjoying the fake feeling of inflated superiority. "We've got a great team—the best. And we're happy to have you on it. I've heard good things about you. Is it true you landed a seven-figure deal in your first three months with Stockwell?"

And it was as easy as that.

I spent a decent thirty minutes fielding questions about myself, playing up how much better their city was, and they were all ready to be my new best friend.

Not everyone was as easy to placate as my new friend, Peter, trying their best to tease out of me a little more personal information than I was prepared to give. But it wasn't my first rodeo. Nope, I gave them enough so they didn't think I was being evasive but kept all the best parts under lock and key.

In the meantime, Sarah sipped on a fucking Diet Coke or some other bullshit "non-alcoholic" drink and pretended like she wasn't watching.

Actually, it wasn't even watching, it was more like studying. Her brown eyes moved in careful calculation across the room, shifting back to me with each new addition to my conversational circle. I could almost see the notes she was mentally taking as her promise of just-one-drink melted into another.

Yeah. I thought so.

She didn't want to leave just yet.

I turned my attention to some of the women who'd joined us, doing my best not to be rude.

"Crystal, right?" I tipped my glass in her direction. "You set my password up for me." I slowly brought the glass to my lips.

She'd also been one of the women outside in the hall with Sarah the day I came to visit B&B but bringing that up wouldn't win me any favors.

"Yeah, that was me." Her cheeks pinked as she nodded slowly. "If you have any computer issues, I'm your girl."

"I'll be sure to remember that." I gave her a slow smile.

And where sports analogies and bravado worked on men, being attentive is what was required for women. They didn't need their egos stroked or their town championed, they preferred you looked them in the eye and listened. Novel approach for some men, but it worked like a charm.

Lucky for me I was fluent in both.

Hmmm. And what do you know? The Diet Coke in Sarah's hand looked like it had been switched out to a dirty martini.

Mmmm. Naughty Sarah it seemed was making an appearance.

Cue my complete lack of surprise.

While she might want to project this image as a stiff, white shirt who liked to follow the rules, I knew different. And it made me smile, content I had a secret cache of Sarah knowledge that most of these other suckers had no idea about. Bet no one knew she liked having her hair pulled, or that she'd pulled mine while I went down on her. Or that she was loud when she came and wasn't the china doll she looked to be.

No, she kept that part of herself locked up tight, granting me access only because she assumed she'd never see me again. And damn me if I wasn't hoping to get another peek.

Her tongue swiped across her lips in a move she probably hadn't intended to be sexy. But any man who'd seen it would argue otherwise and I had most definitely seen it.

See, I was strategically maintaining my distance while keeping her in my line of sight. Because as much as she wanted to see me, I most definitely wanted to see her. And unlike where she positioned herself, I didn't even have to try, able to see every tick of her agitated jaw with very little effort.

And that was how it would stay, vowing to not make a move tonight. There wasn't a chance I was going to make her do anything she didn't want to do. Which was why I stayed on my side of the bar, making sure she didn't feel threatened while feeding into her curiosity about me.

And I knew she was curious.

It wasn't arrogance either—okay not all arrogance—because I wasn't stupid.

Just like I'd made some inquiries about her, I'd be disappointed if she hadn't done the same for me.

Found out where I went to school, where I'd used to live—all the mundane boring stuff that made me look good on paper.

But she didn't need a file of bullshit to know who I was, she'd seen that firsthand months ago with her own two eyes.

She blinked, seeing that I'd caught her watching me and it made me smile.

It had been a while since I played cat and mouse.

And wasn't I enjoying the hell out of it.

8

Sarah

"LOOK AT THEM." I ROLLED my eyes at Crystal and Maggie, both of them fawning over Kyle like cats in heat. "Could they be any more obvious?"

I should have left.

Had my stupid soda, said my goodbyes and then forgone the rest of this silly spectacle. But nooooooooo, I stupidly talked myself into staying, convinced I could learn something from watching him in his natural habitat. And what I was learning was, I didn't like it.

Heat traveled up my neck and my skin started to sweat. Then came the need for something a little stronger than soda, and I ordered a martini. Which was plain dumb considering the high alcohol content.

"Bah, they don't get out a lot." Kennedy waved off their behavior, ignoring the spectacle and taking a sip of yet another appletini. "Enjoy your drink, and enjoy the fact that they want to go where you've already been."

"Ewww, Kennedy." The martini started to perform as prescribed as I relaxed a little. "I didn't want to be thinking about that."

He was so freaking smooth.

The high top was positioned at a safe distance away. Close enough to still be social, but not so close we could hear the conversations. Which was a blessing and a curse as I watched the laughing and private jokes unfold in front of me. Even Joanna, who'd initially been sitting with us, had jumped ship, making some bullshit excuse about needing the bathroom before skedaddling away to join in the fray.

"Gah, I hate it." I shook my head and took another swallow from my glass. "Easing from one conversation to the next seamlessly. All of them," I waved roughly to the crowd surrounding him. *"Can I order you a drink, Kyle?"* I mimicked their ridiculous display. *"Can I kiss your ass, Kyle?"*

"Ha!" Kennedy laughed. "The last one I'd totally volunteer for myself."

"Actually, his ass is pretty spectacular," I lamented, tipping my glass upside down and noticing the contents had been completely drained. "If you were going to kiss one, it's a good one to kiss."

"Kiss what?" Kyle smirked, conveniently maneuvering himself close enough to catch the tail end of the conversation. Actually, just as well it hadn't been the start—that could have been awkward.

"Nothing you'd be interested in." My hand playfully batted at his chest. Mmm firm. Exactly how I'd remembered it.

"Why don't you let me be the judge of that?" He pulled the empty glass from my hand and set it down on a nearby table.

"Uh-oh," Kennedy laughed. "Sounds to me like someone has his grumpy pants on." Her features animated as she pulled a funny face.

"Kennedy." He purred her name like a sleepy lion, forcing her head to snap up in attention.

"Why don't you get us another round of drinks, my credit card is at the bar."

"Sure, of course." She nodded, falling victim to his magical charm. I was surprised she only agreed to go get the drinks and didn't offer to do it naked. "I'll be right back."

And she was gone.

Damn it.

"Do women always do what you want?" I asked, feeling a little looser now the martini had worked its way into my bloodstream.

"Usually." He didn't hesitate, his cocky grin coming out to play.

"I won't." The words slipped out of my mouth defiantly. "I won't do what you want."

Ha! He might be able to flash his magic smile and get everyone else to fall over themselves, but I wouldn't fall victim. Nope, I would be resistant.

He leaned closer, his lips brushing against my ear, his hot breath against my skin. "That just makes me want you more."

Dirty.

Playing dirty he was, with those sultry, sexy words coming out of those sultry, sexy lips.

I didn't move, taking in a deep breath and sniffing the heady mix of scotch and cologne as I listed all the reasons why kissing him would be a bad idea.

1. I hate him, 2. Maybe hate is a really strong word, maybe . . .

"Kennedy is going to be back soon," I warned, counting on her not being distracted at the bar.

"Good, she can watch."

Those words, while innocent enough on their own, couldn't have been more obscene if they'd tried. I was turned on and wanting him to touch me and not in a way that was even remotely platonic.

I wanted him to kiss me. To pull me off the stool I was perched on and rub himself against me. I wanted his hands everywhere, especially between my legs, where I was aching for him to touch me.

It had to be the booze.

It was the only explanation, because I had never been interested in public displays of affection.

"You are so full of shit." I laughed, bravery I didn't usually possess outside of a boardroom finding its way outside of my mouth.

"Well now." His smile was slow, almost taunting. "I'm going to have to prove it."

I wasn't sure how but in one quick move I was off the stool I'd been sitting on and standing on my feet. The arm around my waist was probably a clue I hadn't gotten that way myself, but it had been so fast, it took a minute to register.

"Walk," he said, motioning for my feet to cooperate and do what they were supposed to. "Unless you want a scene and then I'll happily carry you."

"Whatever," I hissed but didn't stop the one foot in front of the other. "I think you're bluffing."

To be honest, I wasn't so sure. And more to the point, I wasn't sure I wanted him to be.

Hell, maybe what we needed was just to have sex, get it out of our system, and move on. Probably not the rational thing to do but considering I'd been rational and it wasn't working out for me, maybe I needed to do the opposite.

Or maybe even one drink when I was in Kyle's presence was too much. Considering after two I married him, I should definitely not have another.

"Keep walking, sweetheart," he breathed into my ear. "I'm far from bluffing."

This wasn't some dingy bar, the classy establishment was filled with men in business suits and women in pencil skirts, none of which who were paying us any attention.

It felt so illicit, so unlike me and yet I didn't want to stop.

Not yet at least.

By the time we'd reached the employee bathroom, I wasn't sure I'd be able to stop. He pulled open the door and pushed me inside against the wall. His body pressed firm against me.

"Now, who's bluffing?" he whispered, dragging his nose up against mine.

Something inside of me snapped. My mouth found his before he had a chance to find mine and I clawed at him to get closer.

He kissed me back hard as his hands moved lower, grabbing my ass and pushing me higher against the bathroom wall.

It was a frenzy of lips and hands, and bodies dry humping.

While one of his hands held me steady the other hiked up my skirt so that it bunched up around my waist. And with my panties exposed, he moved his attention to my shirt, with amazing—and what I believed to be super human—agility unbuttoning it to reveal my demi cup bra.

Thank God it hadn't been laundry day, and I was wearing my nice lingerie.

"Yes." The word moaned out of me as he lifted my leg to get a better angle. The bulge in his pants did an amazing job at hitting me right where I needed it. "Yes."

I'd never had sex in a public place.

Never wanted to.

But here I was in a bathroom a few feet away from people I worked with, and an unsecured door, ready to have a relative stranger make me come.

What the hell was I doing? And why the hell wasn't I stopping?

"Tell me to stop, Sarah." His mouth moved to my neck as his hands moved to between my legs. "Tell me to stop or I'm not going to."

"Don't stop."

His mouth moved back to mine, his tongue teasing apart my lips as his hard-on rocked against me. Every part of my skin goose bumped, my nipples pressing against the lace of my bra dying for his hand or mouth to touch them. They knew what was coming and were desperate to be kissed, licked, touched, savored—in every way.

"Fuck, I want you." He sucked hard against my throat as his hand pulled aside my panties and plunged two fingers inside of me. "I love the feel of you."

It felt different from our night in Vegas—hotter, more intense. My body amped up from the memory, craving what it knew he would do to me.

"I love the feel of you too," I answered lamely as my hips swirled against his hand, the sweet friction making me so wet I was dangerously close to coming.

So close.

I was so close and I wasn't even naked.

After all, the foreplay had been happening all afternoon and I was so primed it was almost embarrassing.

His mouth moved to my breast, pulling down the lace with his teeth and then flicking my nipple with his tongue. And with his fingers still inside, he used the heel of his palm to circle my clit in an overload of stimulation I had no hope of resisting.

"Kyle!" My legs started to shake as I exploded around his hand. "I'm coming."

He didn't stop, teasing every last ounce of pleasure out of me as I struggled to remain standing.

It hadn't taken long, a few minutes at most and he had reduced me to a hot mess.

"Mmmm, I liked that." He slowly removed his hand from inside my panties and pulled my skirt down. "So sweet." He lifted his fingers to his mouth and sucked them as I watched.

"I-I—"

Yeah, I wasn't sure what I wanted or needed to say, but words weren't my friends right now, my body still struggling to remain upright.

"You were amazing." His lips pressing softly against mine. "And I would love to continue, but I'm not fucking you here."

"Yeah, we shouldn't do that." My head shook even though it wasn't convinced as I tried to button up my blouse. I didn't possess the same dexterity it seemed, my hands fumbling. So much for me *not* doing what he wanted, I'd really shown him. My willpower and resistance were clearly non-existent.

"Get yourself cleaned up, I'll see you out there in a few minutes." He turned on the faucet and washed his hands, completely ignoring the very obvious erection we still hadn't taken care of.

"What about—" My eyes lowered to his hips, my tongue unconsciously sliding across my lips as I contemplated.

His lips twisted, his smile slow as he dried off his hands with a paper towel and stalked closer.

"This?" He moved, rubbing his hard length against me. His

jaw tightened as he sucked in a breath. "What about it?"

"Shouldn't we?" I closed my eyes enjoying the weight of him on me, his scent intoxicating me. "I could . . ."

"Later." He stopped, kissing my nose before pulling away. His body tensed in a display of subhuman control. "See you out there."

And with a flick of his wrist he tossed the paper towel into the wastepaper basket and walked out.

Gone.

What?

What!

How could he walk away? I was a hot mess and I knew he was turned on, I'd felt how hard he was, seen the heat in his eyes. How could he just . . . resist? Was he proving a point?

I was so fucking confused.

9

kyle

I WONDERED IF IT WERE possible to lose the function of your dick.

Fairly sure if there were such a condition, I was dangerously close to being afflicted.

It took an iron will to walk out and leave her there.

Even more so not to go into the men's room and jerk off.

But my cock wasn't craving my hand, so while it would have taken the edge off, I wasn't going to be even close to satisfied by the empty orgasm.

It was like my own personal brand of self-flagellation.

And clearly I had lost my mind.

My intention when I'd approached her was to call a truce of sorts. Not that I had any intention of backing down, but I wasn't going to go out of my way to incite her either.

The road to hell was paved with good intentions.

All it took was her smart mouth, daring me to kiss her. And I never was one to walk away from a dare. Maybe it was a character flaw or a freaking blessing, but her consent was all it took to make me unravel.

And there I was thinking I'd kept it all together.

But thankfully I hadn't lost all my self-control, giving her what she needed before I reined it in.

My dick didn't share in the gratitude.

Unsurprisingly, after Sarah exited the bathroom and rejoined the group, she made her apologies, deciding to leave.

Headache.

Long day / early morning.

Or some other such bullshit.

I swallowed another mouthful of scotch and let the evening come to its natural conclusion before heading back to my apartment, alone.

Crystal had very kindly offered to help me find my way back. In case my sense of direction was lacking, or my dick needed to be sucked. She hadn't clarified which. But in a move that shocked us both, I turned her down.

What had also been shocking was that I hadn't had sex since I'd moved. Originally I chalked it up to lack of opportunity, getting laid not really a priority when you're moving and starting a new job. But it became evident that the blame lay with lack of interest, and my dry spell was more likely self-imposed. Which was a first as far as I could remember.

And the revelations continued.

It was sometime after midnight when my phone buzzed. Its obnoxious vibrating pulled me from what I had been telling myself was sleep. It wasn't. But my eyes had been shut so I figured it was close enough to classify.

"Hello." I didn't bother checking the caller ID.

Anyone who was calling me this late was either blood related or a woman I'd fucked at some point. Either way, evasion wasn't my thing.

"Kyle, it's Sarah."

Hmmm. Well, the night—assuming it wasn't already morning—just took an interesting turn.

"Miss me already?" I smiled into the phone, a little too pleased by the call.

I might have come to the realization that I wasn't interested in anyone else but her, but I wasn't about to give her the upper hand either. Besides, I very much enjoyed the game we played.

"I thought. . . I was thinking. . . ." She tried twice unsuccessfully to finish her sentence before taking a deep breath. "Look, we should talk about what happened."

I could see her almost as clearly as if she were sitting in front of me. The weight of her brown eyes as she contemplated. Probably still wearing last night's clothes as she sat on the edge of her bed.

"How long have you been deliberating whether to call me?" I was genuinely curious. Wondering what else had been going on in her beautiful head.

"Only two hours."

"Two hours?" I smirked into the dark as I stretched out under the sheets. "I would have figured longer."

"Well . . ." She paused. Yeah, I figured there was more to it. "I spent all the time before that wondering if I should come see you instead. By the time I'd decided, I realized I didn't actually know where you live and it was really late. So that's when the call debate started."

"So, what was your decision?"

"Well, I'm on the phone, aren't I? Obviously I called." She

laughed.

"No, I meant about coming and seeing me." I was fairly sure I knew the answer, but I was egotistical and wanted the confirmation. "Assuming you had my address."

"Oh. Well." She paused before adding confidently, "I was going to come."

"You know I would have made sure of it."

"I didn't mean like that."

"No, but I did."

"Just be serious for a second, okay. Because I need to process what the fuck happened." She took a breath and continued before I had a chance to interrupt. "No one knows what went down in that bathroom. No one. Well, obviously you do on account you participated, but other than that I haven't told a soul. Even Kennedy, who eyed me suspiciously when I came back slightly disheveled from my mysterious bathroom expedition and didn't get the scoop."

I pushed back the sheets, my voice getting serious. "And you're worried I'm going to talk?"

"No. No of course not." She sighed, and something in my chest loosened that she knew that I wouldn't. "I'm just not sure whether to file it away under a psychotic episode or demonic possession. I'm not sure which of those categories makes me less of a basket case."

Fuck, it was a genuine mystery how the hell she could be so adorable and sexy at the same time.

"I'll clear it up for you." I took a breath. "I'm in my bed, naked, and I can't think of a good enough reason why you're not in it with me."

If she'd expected anything other than the truth, she would be sadly mistaken.

"The lack of address would probably be the reason."

I laughed.

I couldn't help it.

She was truly extraordinary.

Not only was she sexy and smart, but I'd already slept with her and was still interested. I wasn't sure I'd come across that combination in . . . Well, I *hadn't* come across that combination.

"Sarah."

"Kyle."

"I'll give you my address. Now come to my bed."

10

Sarah

WHAT DO YOU CALL A one-night stand you sleep with again?

It sounded like a joke missing a punch line.

Was it crazy?

Was I?

We were consenting adults. Who'd had good sex. Actually it was more like freaking amazing sex. Which wasn't typical considering I'd been an adult for a while and had a lot of *average* sex, but not so much *amazing*. So didn't I owe it to myself to have great sex when I could? And now we sort of knew each other—or getting to know each other, as was the case—so the danger of him being a psychopath was considerably reduced.

Plus we had been, and would continue to, be responsible. There would be no *"oops, I'm pregnant"* or *"hey, does this rash look normal to you?"* I was on the pill and we would use condoms, because, safety first.

He answered the door of his loft apartment wearing a pair of sweatpants that had no business being that sexy. "You're not naked." I took a step inside and unbuttoned my coat.

"I'm trying to keep the public indecency charges to a minimum.

I just moved in." He smirked, pulling me closer and ignoring my battle to undress.

"This isn't going to change anything at work." I kept talking as his lips started to get busy on my neck. His fingers also found their purpose and managed to get me out of my coat and start on the buttons of my blouse. Seriously impressive those fingers of his. "We are going to do this and it won't get weird."

"It won't get weird." His lips moved down my chest as my blouse fell to the floor.

"This is totally okay." I'm not sure why I was still talking; I had already kicked off my heels, my bare feet returning to the floor. "And this isn't me doing what you want. I'm here because *I* want it. There is a distinction."

Yes.

His hands moved across me, touching my skin, every inch of me on fire.

Oh God, *yes.*

This was my doing, not his.

I was still in control.

"A very clear distinction, which I'm happy you're on board with." His fingers and mouth did things that didn't seem humanly possible.

"God, you're a good kisser," I moaned as, with a quick flick across my back, my bra disappeared. "I made the right call coming here."

"Yeah, you did." He stopped kissing me, grabbed me roughly and hauled me over his shoulder.

My world turned upside down, literally, as I dangled. My legs secured by his hands as he strode confidently to what I assumed was his bedroom.

No prelude.

Like a caveman, with me—the cavewoman presumably—in a fireman hold as we moved through his apartment, hitting the light switch as light flooded the room.

"What are you doing?" I wriggled, only half of me undressed.

"Having sex with my wife."

"I'm not—"

I didn't get to finish the sentence, my equilibrium again tilted as he flipped me onto his mattress.

With a tug, those obscene sweatpants dropped to the floor and he was standing in front of me, naked.

Kyle clothed was impressive. He clearly worked out, with toned, defined muscles in the right places. But stripped, with all that in view—he was spectacular.

He had a body that deserved its own monument. And when he looked at me the way he was looking—eyes hooded, with so much intent I thought I might actually burst—I completely understood the arrogance.

"What were you saying?" His hand lowered to his rock-hard length as he gave it a stroke. "You aren't . . .?"

"Naked." I fumbled with the zipper at the back of my skirt, desperate to get it off.

"No, you aren't."

He watched as I won my battle with the skirt and then slid my underwear off, my body completely bare in front of him.

I had never been this exposed before, not having the confidence in my own skin he seemed to. The harsh halogen of the overhead chandelier seemed so severe, displaying every imperfection. But as he watched me, I didn't cower or cover any part of me.

There was no need to impress him. I felt a confidence I hadn't felt before, giving myself permission to show him what I had been afraid to show other men. With him, it just felt different. The way he looked at my body made me feel like a goddess.

"Spread your legs," he ordered, stroking his cock slowly as he grabbed a condom from the nightstand. We watched each other. Me, as he tore open the packet and covered himself with it, and him, as my thighs parted on his command. "Mmm. Very nice."

I'd never done this. Sex with the lights on with no pretense. And it felt like it was something beyond sex. Almost scandalous but wow, did it feel hotter than hell. I wasn't sure what had changed, but I liked the way it felt.

The way *I* felt.

"I want you inside of me." I spoke words I'd never said out loud.

"You're in luck, sweetheart." He grabbed my legs and pulled me further down the mattress, my butt resting on the edge. "Because that's where I'm going to be."

With his big hands holding my legs open, he pushed inside in one hard thrust, barely giving me time to adjust. A sting of slight pain bit at me as he stopped and pulled out halfway, his thumb moving to circle my clit.

He was large, bigger than what I was used to, filling me again as he thrust deep. "You're beautiful."

It was the first time a man ever said that to me and I didn't argue.

I didn't even speak.

I think I might have lost the ability all together.

Instead, I arched my back, giving myself to him as he controlled the tempo.

Deeper.

Harder.

Faster.

His thick cock pulled out of me for a second, using the opportunity to flip me onto my stomach suddenly and slapping my ass as he lifted it in the air. I moaned as his hard length filled me again.

"I thought about this the whole time I fingered you in that bathroom." He fucked me from behind as I scrambled on all fours.

"While I drank my scotch."

Faster.

"On my way home."

Harder.

"When I jerked off in the shower because I couldn't take it anymore."

Deeper.

His fingers moved to my clit, circling as he continued to thrust, my hips rocking back to meet him as I struggled to stay on my knees.

"I thought about this right here." His fingers twisted my clit, the pressure sending an orgasm rocketing through my body as I gasped out loud.

Barely remaining upright, every nerve tingling through my body as he continued his assault.

"That's it, sweetheart. You feel so amazing when you come."

Relentless waves crashed over me as he grabbed my waist and pumped into me, my pussy pulsing against his thick cock as I screamed out his name.

"Kyle. Yes. Yes. Yes."

"Yes, baby. I'm right here." There was one last thrust and then he stilled, exploding into me as I collapsed.

"Right here." He started to move again slowly, his cock jerking with each rock of his hips. "God, you feel good."

My body shook as he pulled out, rolling onto his side and joining me on the mattress.

"Mmm. Better than I remembered." I felt his smile against my skin as his arms wrapped around me and lifted me further up the bed. "Don't even think about leaving."

"I'm not." I nodded, too exhausted to move. "But not because you want me to."

"Yeah, yeah. Free will. Your choice. Whatever you need to tell yourself." He laughed, pulling me closer against him and kissed my neck. "Give me a second to clean up."

The mattress dipped as he turned, lifting himself off the bed and turning off the light. Tiny white spots appeared in the blackness while my eyes adjusted as I heard him move through the room.

I rolled onto my side, my sight returning as I followed his shadow into an adjoining bathroom.

The pop of a light switch.

The faucet.

The water running.

Then the padding of feet as I watched him return.

"Open for me." He knelt on the bed with a soft warm towel in his hand and carefully wiped between my thighs. A smile spread across his face as he gently patted me dry. "You're so compliant after sex. I'll need to remember that."

"And *you* are extremely cocky." I rolled my eyes.

"I'm like that all the time."

And wasn't that the truth.

He dumped the towel and crawled back into bed. My body instinctively nestled closer to him, which was weird since I wasn't usually a cuddler. It's like parts of me remembered how good it felt in Vegas, he'd been a stranger then—not sure he was much more now—but it just somehow felt right.

Ugh.

I was overthinking.

"What are you thinking about?"

He had to have a sixth sense. His intuition was way too astute.

"I've never done casual sex before."

Like my body had slipped into Vegas habits, so had my mouth. It was easy to talk to him; the idea of never having to see him again gave me permission to not hold back. It was something I had never done in relationships. Not just sexual ones, but in all areas of my life. Of course that theory was now a bust, I was not only going to have to see him *repeatedly* but also work with him. And yet strangely, that feeling of ease remained.

"I know. Which is why you waited until *after* our ceremony the first time."

"What?" I twisted around to face him, my mind now more full of questions than answers. "What do you mean?"

"I mean we met at a bar. We could have easily had sex in a bathroom like we almost did at The Waiting Room, I'm almost positive that's like a rite of passage in Vegas. But you didn't even kiss me until after that asshole in the white jumpsuit pronounced us husband and wife. Intellectually you knew it was casual, but I think subconsciously you needed something to feel like it wasn't. It was like you were giving yourself permission."

Oh. My. God.

I froze in silence, barely able to breathe.

How could a man I barely knew be able to see that about me so clearly? What's more I couldn't even get defensive and argue, telling him he was wrong. If I was honest, really and truly honest, I knew he was right.

"God." I hid my head in the crook of his neck. "What the hell is wrong with me?"

"Nothing." He brought me in closer, his hand rubbing circles on my back. "Why the hell do you think there is something wrong?"

"Because." I was wondering whether I should just save us both the time and put together a Power Point display. The reasons were bound to be numerous. "I tried to have a hook up, and even then I screwed it up."

"Sarah, do you see anyone complaining here?" He tried to lift my head, I resisted, for the first time since meeting him feeling incredibly embarrassed.

"You dated a guy for years, and you were supposed to get married. And before that you probably only had sex with a steady boyfriend," he continued, accurately guessing my dating history. "You aren't going to turn around in one night and go fuck some random dude without a reason. Even if the reason was basically smoke and mirrors."

"So, why did *you* do it?" I lifted my head, looking him in the eye. Sure, he'd been right about my motivations, but that didn't explain his participation. I'm surprised he didn't run in the opposite direction. "Seems like a lot of trouble for sex."

"Actually, it wasn't." He laughed, moving the hair off my face. "You were probably more honest than most women. So we had to go through the charade, big deal. You didn't demand a thing from me. Not before, not during, not after."

"But you said," I know I didn't imagine it, "you are the opposite of me. You rarely had girlfriends. You're like the serial one-night stand guy."

As I'd been honest with him, he'd been honest with me. For all the years I'd put into trying to build and maintain a perfect relationship, he'd happily screwed around. I didn't judge him, why the hell should I? And hey, if I was going to reap the benefit of those years with what he gave me in bed, then I sure as hell wasn't about to complain. But why—and this was where it made no sense—would a guy who boasted his preference for no strings, go through with a wedding—even if it was a sham—for a one-night stand?

"You see, most people can't do the casual thing in any capacity. They say they can and then they inevitably want more. You didn't even ask for my number. So what, I had to jump through a few hoops so you felt okay about it. Trust me, it wasn't a hardship. You were the most honest girl I'd probably ever met."

"This is so messed up." I laughed. "Like so, so very, very messed up."

"No, it's not." He softly brushed his lips against mine. "Now, get some sleep. You know how I feel about morning sex."

"Yeah, I remember." I was sure I was going to be walking funny as well. "I like your morning sex."

"Good. So sleep."

11

Kyle

"HELLO?"

The sound of her voice broke through like a sort of dream. I'd slept better than I had in a long time. Great sex will do that, and it had been a really long time since I'd had the kind that gave me that kind of exhaustion. Since leaving Vegas to be exact.

"Sorry, no. I'm really sorry. I'm . . . a friend."

Well, that woke me, my eyes sliding open to see Sarah sitting up in bed in a panic.

"Um. Yes. Wait. Hang on. I'll get him." She held the phone out in front of her like it had suddenly developed teeth. Her head shook as she mouthed the words, "Sorry, I thought it was mine."

"Hello," I answered, not concerned she'd answered my phone.

I didn't have a secret double life, and she was aware I'd been far from a good boy so whoever was on the other side of that call was no threat to me. Again, evasive wasn't in my repertoire.

"Kyle Mathew Drake."

It was Keely, earlier than I was used to hearing her I might add. But it was a Tuesday, and she would assume I'd be heading to work by eight, so a seven a.m. phone call was not suspicious.

"Three names, someone's upset."

"Don't even start with me. You have a *girlfriend* and didn't tell me? How long has this been going on? What's her name? When do I get to meet her?" She fired out questions barely taking a breath, her voice hitching on excitement and a little anger no doubt. My sister had enough emotions for the both of us.

"If you want answers you should pause between questions." My hand moved to Sarah's arm, pulling her back into bed.

She'd probably assumed I wanted privacy and was attempting to get out of bed. But I already told her to expect morning sex and regardless of the phone call, *that* was happening.

"Fine, answers." She huffed into the phone. "Why didn't you tell me you had a girlfriend?"

I could have easily told Keely that Sarah was just a girl who had spent the night. It would have still invited more questions because I didn't usually let my female friends answer my phone, but I was confident it would have appeased her.

Of course, what I had in front of me was an opportunity that I found too good to pass up.

"Sarah's not my girlfriend." My eyes shifted to her, watching her reaction as I smiled. "She's the woman I married in Vegas."

There was a sharp intake of air on either side of the phone, one from my sister, the other from Sarah, her eyes peeled back to maximum capacity.

You'd think it would get old, but I secretly loved watching her on edge. Sarah I meant. I guess, Keely as well. Perhaps I was just an all-around bastard. And if I was, it wouldn't be changing soon.

"What are you doing?" Sarah whispered, the fire in her eyes making my cock twitch. "Stop telling people that."

It was ridiculous how much her reaction excited me. I was probably never going to stop.

"Kyle!" Keely finding her words as she launched into what I assumed would be one of her epic tongue-lashings. "I swear on Mom and Dad's grave, if you're telling the truth . . . If you got married . . . And if this is a joke . . . What the hell?"

"I tried to tell you, you didn't listen." I smirked, Sarah's brow knitting in confusion. "In any case, this should alleviate your concerns about me needing a wife. I have one, she's wonderful and I need to be at work in two hours, so I have husbandly duties I need to perform. Talk soon."

I hung up, tossing the phone on the bed beside me. After all, I was a man of my word and the clock was ticking.

"Are you insane? Who the hell are you telling we're married?" She pushed roughly against my chest as I moved in to kiss her. "I'm not going to be used as an excuse for you to ward off an old girlfriend. I'm going to kill you."

Yeah, it never got old.

Her annoyance was like an aphrodisiac. More so because I knew I brought it out in her. No other man had gotten that, I was sure of it. This was just for me.

"It's probably unhealthy how turned on I get when you're angry, but she's not my ex-girlfriend. She's my sister."

"Then why would you tell her that?" She continued to swat at my chest, her anger showing no signs of receding.

She was hot as hell, her face wild, with untamed hair, and eyes full of fury.

"Because she needs to stop meddling in my personal life, and I already told you, it gets me hard."

I grabbed her hand and moved it to my cock. She seemed like she'd appreciate the visual cue, and I liked her hand there. "Like that."

"You probably woke up like that." I removed my hand, but she kept hers against my shaft, palming me as she spoke. "Probably had nothing to do with me."

"You know it did." I leaned back allowing her a better angle. "And more importantly, you like that it did."

It was useless to argue. Whether she liked to admit it or not, I knew her better than she knew herself.

"I need to go home and change before work, I don't have time for this." She continued to stroke me.

"I can be quick, give you time to go home and change." I moved in closer, my lips owning hers. "Or I can be slow and we can be late."

The choice was hers because I knew that she needed it. But make no mistake, we weren't leaving my apartment until I'd made her come at least once.

And with a smile she said the word I was hoping for.

"Slow."

We arrived thirty minutes late.

I drove us to her place so she could change, which meant now I had her address too.

Her apartment was exactly how I expected it to be, neat, well-decorated and in a decent part of town. I also knew she lived alone, her limp-dick ex fiancé—her last roommate. I'd heard about his recent legal troubles, not my doing, but I can't say it didn't make me smile.

And while it was tempting to see how her mattress compared to mine, I was conscious we were on the clock. So I let her get dressed, confident I would get to *undress* her later.

No one noticed we were either late or had arrived together, something I knew she had been concerned about. We were discussing the latest financials as we exited the elevator so to the untrained eye it looked like we had arrived from a meeting. Ironically, it hadn't been choreographed, she'd pulled up one of the files after she'd gotten home from the bar in an effort to distract her from the should-I-stay-or-should-I-go argument. And while she was stalling the inevitable she'd noticed a discrepancy in the numbers. The shared car ride to the office gave her the opportunity to bring it to my attention. And what worked out to be the perfect cover also meant we had saved our client about fifteen percent. Even better was that she asked for my input. Something she would never have done the day before.

We didn't discuss sex at work.

That was hard—and I do mean *hard*—on multiple levels.

For one, she was freaking gorgeous. There was something about seeing her all buttoned up and locked down that flipped a switch in me I had no hope of ignoring. And even if I could ignore all the exterior hotness, I didn't stand a chance when it came to her freaking mind.

She was brilliant, a consummate professional, driving through the day with a focus and determination that demanded respect. She looked people in the eye when she spoke, said what she meant, and didn't back down.

And I didn't think I could get any harder than when she told

Logan from PR to give us revisions because his first submission was bullshit.

"What are you doing?" she asked, watching me close the door as Logan left with his tail between his legs.

I might have felt sorry for him except I was too fucking pleased with the results. "Saving the rest of the office from seeing this." I pointed to the bulge in the front of my pants.

Her eyes darted down, widening with understanding. "How did that happen?" She pushed a stray strand of her hair out of the way with an innocent smile I knew wasn't sincere.

Christ.

If I hadn't already had all the blood in my body flowing south, that coy little smile of hers would have done it.

"You know *how* that happened." I strode to the desk with purpose, unsure whether I wanted to have her straddle me in a chair or bend her over the desk. Both had their benefits.

Her eyes swung to the door, lifting to her feet just as I closed the distance between us. "We can't, what if someone hears us?" The warmth of her palm radiated through my shirt as she rested it on my chest.

Valid point.

My wife liked to get vocal, especially when I made her come as hard as I was intending to. "What if I gag you?" I pinched her ass, bringing her closer so she could see what she was doing to me. "I've been looking for an excuse to take this tie off all day."

"Hmmm, really?" She inched up her leg, giving me more contact. Her eyes had darkened, biting her lip while she flirted with the HR policy and me.

I didn't need confirmation that it was her first time doing

something other than work in her office; her hesitation said everything her words didn't.

Before either of us got a chance to explore how far she was willing to go, there was a knock at the door, breaking the moment.

She dropped her leg to the floor, simultaneously straightening her skirt as she took a step back. Not that she had to worry about her clothes, her flaming cheeks betrayed more than the slightly rumpled fabric.

"Let me go see who that is. Why don't you sit down and try to not look like you were about to let me defile your desk."

"I—" she cleared her throat, shaking her head. "Maybe it was *me* who was about to defile *you*."

I laughed—couldn't help it—amused she thought that was what would've happened. Grabbing a file from her desk to cover my erection, I strode to the door to see who I was going to hate for the interruption.

"Kyle." Adele looked surprised to see me. "Is everything okay in here?" She looked to Sarah for confirmation.

Shit, it was one of the bosses.

"Yep, everything is fine." Sarah straightened in her chair, managing to lose the blush as she locked eyes with Adele. "Kyle and I were just going over a campaign, why do you ask?"

It was no secret that Adele adored Sarah—can't say that I blamed her—and if one of us were to go, I would be her first choice. She wasn't overt in showing it, but looking to Sarah for an explanation spoke volumes.

"When I saw Logan in the hall he said things were tense in here. I just want to make sure everyone is working as part of the team. We very much value collaboration here at B&B." Her eyes swung to me for the last part.

The irony.

Collaborating was exactly what I was trying to do when she knocked on the door. Not sure it fell in line with her vision of team, but it sure as hell did with mine.

"Logan felt "tension" because his presentation was subpar," I offered, which wasn't a lie. Unless he was talking about the sexual tension, in which case, I had nothing.

Sarah rose to her feet before adding her part. "Like Kyle said, we were dissatisfied with what he put together and asked he re-submit. As far as the two of us working together." She stopped, biting her lip as she glanced at me to stop herself from smiling. "We've settled into a . . . routine."

I bit back the grin, her pause hilarious considering I knew exactly what that *routine* involved.

Adele took a minute, evaluating us both as she tried to work out if Sarah was full of shit. I had no doubt she wasn't buying it completely, but the evidence in front of her didn't give her much choice.

Sarah hadn't crumbled, the blush hadn't crept back on her face and she looked every bit convincing as she held her head high.

I had a hunch that underneath all that external bravado she was panicking, not that anyone else would see that. Nope, her silent confidence sent a shiver right down to my balls.

Fuck me.

There was no way I would ever get enough of that.

"Thanks Adele for the concern, but we're all good here." I tipped my head to the door. "I'm going to go chase up the Lotus account with the social media department and see where they're at. Sarah, when you have a moment." My eyes clashed with hers. "Please come to my office so we can finish what we started earlier. I don't like leaving projects unfinished." And making my wife come was one project I was incredibly keen to complete.

She swallowed, knowing exactly what I meant and gave me a curt nod. "I'll see what I can do Kyle, I have some things to take care of first."

Unless those *things* included removing her panties and making herself wet, I didn't care what she needed to do first. But I was willing to play the game and keep up appearances if that's what she wanted.

"Sure, whenever you're ready." My lips spread into a smile. "I'll be waiting. Ladies, I'll see you both later." My head tipped a goodbye, striding to the door, and taking the file that was covering my hard-on with me.

Adele didn't follow me out, probably wanting to reaffirm with Sarah that everything was fine between us. But I wasn't worried, Sarah could more than hold her own. My only regret, that I wasn't there to see her do it.

Badass Sarah was my kryptonite.

12

Sarah

FOR ALL MY ASSURANCES THAT I had been fine with sharing the promotion, Adele knew different. We never spoke about it because as much as I classified her my friend, she was still my boss. But just like she hadn't enjoyed being paired up with her now husband initially, she could sense my displeasure.

And originally, she'd been right. But currently, I wasn't sure how much of me was still annoyed at the situation.

"Sarah." She was the first one to speak. "Is there anything else you need to add now that Kyle has gone?" Her brow lifted, waiting for me to launch into a debate that a few days ago I'd have no problem delivering.

Amazing what a difference a couple of days could make.

My head shook, doing my best to look her in the eye when I'd been moments away from doing things in my office I'd never imagined doing. "Honestly, it's fine. I'm not going to lie and tell you I was excited about having to share the promotion. But since meeting Kyle and working with him, I can see the benefit for both of us and the company. He's brilliant and ambitious and if I'm honest, will push me harder to do well. There's no need to be concerned."

And for what it was worth, I actually believed it. Not that I didn't want to still prove myself and work my way further up the company. But the hostility, maybe I'd been a little unfair?

Wow.

How did that happen?

I went from sleeping with the enemy to singing his praises, and no one was more surprised than me.

Adele's gaze softened, her lips twitching into a grin. "I'm so pleased." She let out a sigh of relief. "Caleb and I were really hoping you'd work well together and I agree with you. I think everyone will see the benefit. Maybe not Logan." She laughed.

"No, probably not Logan." I chuckled back. "And thanks for believing in me. I know it would have been easy to just give the promotion to someone else, but the fact you have given me this chance means a lot."

Adele held her hands up, putting a stop to my gratitude. "Don't thank anyone but yourself, Sarah. You've done the hard work, you've earned this fair and square. Trust me, no one is doing anyone any favors here."

"Well then, maybe you should wait and see what I have in store because I have a lot more left to show you." I straightened my spine, feeling elevated in my purpose.

"Good. I can't wait."

She said her goodbye and let herself out, leaving me with an empty office and a mind full of confliction.

I was genuinely excited for my future in B&B, and had no doubt that if Kyle and I could keep it professional, we'd achieve great things. I also knew I had an ache between my legs and was dying for him to touch me, wanting to get lost in the moment in a way I'd never been able to before.

I'd been so close.

So close to letting him do whatever he wanted to with people that we worked with just a few feet away.

And as much as I wanted to—to let him take me to that place—it couldn't happen. Not here. Not risk everything I'd built because I was careless.

If we were caught, it would be me who was looked at sideways with judgment. He would no doubt be seen as the office stud, irresistible with his handsome face and godlike body. While I'd be the weak woman who couldn't help but fold like a deck chair at the hint of his smile. I wouldn't allow myself to become a joke, a giggle in the kitchenette and a rumor around the cubicles.

So as much as I wanted to walk into his office and have him put his hands all over me, I wouldn't allow it.

Not here.

With confidence coursing through my veins—and slightly worried I'd lose my nerve if I didn't lay the ground rules first—I moved to my door, stepped into the hall and walked with purpose to his office.

I knocked once, not giving him a chance to reply before I opened the door and let myself in.

He was at his desk, his attention taken from whatever had been on his computer screen as his head lifted and he looked up at me. His eyes were blazing, saying dirty things and still making me feel beautiful. It truly was a gift, his ability to say everything without uttering a word.

"You get everything done?" He pushed away from his desk, not waiting for my answer as he moved toward me and pulled my body closer.

I wanted to kiss him.

His mouth inches from mine while my body melded against his, and I could feel my resolve waning.

"No."

It wasn't loud, a whisper on my lips as I looked him in the eye.

"No?" he asked, tipping his head as if to test it had been the word I'd meant to use.

"Not here." It was surprisingly more convincing than I'd heard it in my head, but as it left my mouth I breathed a sigh of relief. "I had a lot of fun last night and—"

"And I know you aren't going to tell me that it was a one-time deal." He took a slight step back, just enough to break contact. "Because you know that didn't work out so well for us the first time."

Well, he was right about that.

"No, I'm not going to tell you it was a one-time deal." My hands unconsciously rose to his chest, my skin pressed against his trying to get its fix without acting inappropriate. After all, since I had been the one to say "not here" it wouldn't look good for me to break my own rule.

"Then what is it you want, Sarah?" His eyes dropped to my palms pressing against the front of his shirt, bringing them back to mine as he waited for my answer.

I wasn't sure I'd ever been asked what I'd wanted by a man.

Not really.

Not in a way that I felt he cared about my answer.

But as Kyle stood there—exercising incredible restraint—he genuinely looked like he wanted to know.

God, he was sexy.

"I want to do what we did last night again." My voice husky as my thoughts floated back to the hours we'd spent between the sheets. "I want to feel you inside of me, I want to do . . ." *God, I didn't even know what.* "More with you."

His chest rose, a slow breath escaping from his lips as he brought them to my ear. "Then we're on the same page, sweetheart. I want all those things too. I want to watch you ride my cock, to feel you come hard again and again, slowly losing both our minds before we let ourselves go to sleep."

The pull in my lower belly intensified, the need to throw caution out the window at an all-time high.

But I wouldn't.

"Just not here," I warned, the hand against his chest pressing hard against his pectoral.

He shifted back, a smile playing on his lips. "You want to lay some ground rules? Go ahead, I can play nice when motivated."

"Nothing physical at work. No kissing, touching or *accidental rubbing*." My list of demands made their way out of my mouth. "In this building, we are co-workers and nothing else. I don't expect you to treat me any different than anyone else. When the day is done and we walk away from here, then we can do those other things."

His lips pressed together, seeming to be considering it. "So if I was to kiss you right now, stick my hand up your skirt and make you come, that would be breaking your rules? Even though there is no one around to see it?"

The "yes" spoken on a shaking breath. He wasn't making it easier for me, but then again I think that had been his intention.

"Fine." He took a further step back, my hand falling between us as he increased the distance. "Hands and lips will be kept to myself."

"And other parts as well," I added, not wanting him to find the loophole because it hadn't been clarified. "Especially your dick."

His lips busted into a full-blown grin as a low groan blew out of his mouth. "God, I love it when you talk dirty, say it again."

"Kyle," I started to protest knowing that I shouldn't. But there was something in his eyes just daring me to do it, and it made my skin tingle.

Taking a deep breath, I leveled him with a stare as I repeated it. "Especially your *dick*."

His jaw ticked, his hands balling at his side as he fought whatever urge was running through him. "My *dick* as well as the rest of me will respect your wishes, sweetheart. But like you said, when we leave these four walls, that sweet ass of yours is mine."

A shiver ran through me, surprised at how much I liked the sound of his proposition. "Fine, and your *sweet ass* is mine."

"All yours," he agreed without a hint of reservation.

I wasn't sure exactly what having each other's *sweet ass* entailed, but I was excited to find out.

"Well, good." I nodded, wanting desperately to break my own rule and kiss him. "Then I'll see you later."

Without giving either of us a chance at a proper goodbye, I turned on my heel and strode out of his office. With the door closed and me safely on the other side, I breathed a sigh of relief and congratulated myself for being strong.

Don't get me wrong; I'd never been tempted to mix business with pleasure. There hadn't been any men around the office I'd given more than just a curious glance to. And the idea of dating one of them was so foreign I hadn't even considered it. But with Kyle, it was different.

Which was why I needed to keep my head screwed on straight.

Not willing to test myself further, I went back to my office and worked solidly through the day. The times where I did see Kyle, he was a locked vault. His emotions were completely unreadable as he kept all his interactions so professional and above board, I had to wonder if our earlier close encounter had even happened. If I'd prided myself on my self control, then he'd earned the next level admiration. It was intriguing to watch, his attention razor sharp at all times.

But when it was time to leave, he was outside my door waiting.

"Time to go." His head tipped down the hall.

My eyes glanced from side to side, half expecting someone to be looking at us suspiciously but they weren't.

"Sure," I answered as I followed him to the elevator.

No one paid us any mind as they too finished for the day. No second looks passed as we walked out together, and not so much as a raised eyebrow when I hopped into his car.

It was like we were invisible, everyone too preoccupied with their own business to care about what we were doing.

He drove a car like he conducted a meeting, completely in control and with no hesitation. I had been so focused on getting into work without anyone noticing we'd been together I hadn't had a chance to appreciate it earlier.

"Are you a control freak?" I asked, my body relaxing, caressed by his soft leather seats.

His head turned, the smile unmistakably amused as his eyes diverted from the traffic. "You're asking me? Seems like that title is more your thing, don't you think?"

"I never said I wasn't." I shrugged, making no apologies. "I just think you aren't as fancy free as you pretend to be."

He laughed, shaking his head as his attention returned to the road. "I never pretended to be fancy free, baby, that's an assumption you made all by yourself."

Hmmm, well, he was right about that.

Maybe because he'd seemed so much more relaxed and calm, I'd created my own idea of what he was like. But to be honest, I didn't really *know*.

Within the confines of the car, and knowing he had limited opportunity to respond, I felt my confidence grow. "True, but then, you haven't exactly given me a lot to go on."

"What do you want to know?" he volleyed back, nonchalantly. "Ask me anything you want."

I lingered over the question, pondering what exactly I did want to know. There were so many random thoughts that I was surprised when the first question left my lips.

"Have you ever been married?"

Not sure why it was the first thing apparently my mind had decreed as important or why it was even relevant. His past wasn't any of my business, yet as I waited for his answer, I found myself leaning forward in my seat, wanting to know.

He turned, the grin beaming off his face. "Yes, actually I have. Vegas, a few months ago. And my wife won't let me fuck her in my office."

I rolled my eyes, about to correct him for the hundredth time that we hadn't been legally married, when instead I didn't. "Your wife sounds smart. You should probably listen to her more often."

A throaty laugh found its way up his throat. "You're right, she *is* smart. And beautiful, and sexy, along with at least a dozen other things. But right now, I'm not interested in listing the virtues of my wife. I'm more interested in what I'm going to feed her."

My skin flushed, feeling warm all over as I answered as con-fidently as I was able. "Maybe you could start with your dick."

I wasn't sure if I was trying to be funny or seductive, but there was zero amusement when he turned to look at me. His eyes were blazing, his grip on the steering wheel tightened, as his voice dropped to a rumble. "If that's what she wants, it would be my pleasure to give it to her."

Heat bloomed inside of me, my head nodding as I squeezed my knees together. "It's what she wants."

"Then let me get my wife home and make sure she's taken care of."

13

kyle

MY WIFE WAS FULL OF surprises.

I'd expected a game of twenty questions in the car but she'd only managed one. And didn't I enjoy giving her the answer.

But it seemed I wasn't the only one handing out surprises, my wife giving me one of her own. The mention of my dick in her mouth enough to drive me insane.

She didn't ask where I was driving when I took her back to my apartment. No objections were raised when I pulled up her skirt. And not a fucking word was spoken while I fucked her on my dining room table like I'd been dying to do all day. And because I was a man of my word—and only after I'd made her come at least twice—I let her have what she'd asked for in the car. Taking her to my shower, I watched the spray hit our bodies as she sucked my dick.

She undertook the task with such enthusiasm that I struggled not to come. I wanted it to last forever, teetering on the edge while she did amazing things to me with that fucking perfect mouth.

It was a beautiful kind of hell—somewhere between torture and ecstasy—and I reveled in it until my body overrode my mind and I came with a shout. She didn't stop; taking every last drop I had to give her with deep, desperate pulls.

And when she was done, I lifted her off her knees and washed every inch of her body. Wrapped in my best towels, I carried her to my bed where I went down on her until she begged me to stop.

I didn't remember falling asleep, exhaustion taking both of us at some point as I held her in my arms. It was only when my alarm went off that I'd realized we hadn't done anything else.

No dinner.

No conversation.

And no more questions.

Ordinarily I would have called it the perfect night, but there was something lacking as I watched her open her eyes and smile back at me. Something that I couldn't quite place.

"Why are you looking at me like that?" She laughed, curling into my arm and burying her face in my chest.

I lifted her chin, forcing her to look at me. "Don't hide yourself from me, Sarah. I want to see all of you."

"Fine," she huffed, rolling her eyes. "So what were you thinking?"

God she was beautiful.

Her face completely bare, her eyes bright, and hair a tangled cloud of soft blonde curls.

"I was thinking," I pushed the hair out of her eyes, "I'd like to take you out tonight."

"Like a date?" she asked, the word seeming foreign in her mouth. "I thought you didn't date?"

"It's not a date," I corrected her, the notion I'd do it with anyone else seeming to cheapen what I was trying to do with her.

I wasn't sure why exactly, but it was different and I didn't want comparisons drawn from our past by either of us.

"So what are we going to do on this non-date, night out?" Her lips hit my neck, making their way up to my jaw in a succession of small kisses.

"Dinner. A *proper* dinner," I clarified, acutely aware I'd reneged on my intention the day before. "I'll let you pick where."

The kissing stopped, her teeth gently biting my chin as she giggled. "Kind of sounds like a date, Kyle."

"It's not a fucking date," I groaned, no longer feeling like talking, as I took her mouth and hauled her on top of me. She didn't resist, opening her arms and her mouth so I could get the access I was craving.

My tongue invaded her, kissing her as my hands grabbed her ass and squeezed it. Morning sex had always been my plan but I'd expected to multitask it with the shower. We'd already been late the day before, and as much as I preferred walking into my office after both of us thoroughly getting off, two days in a row was pushing it.

Besides, we had her rule to contend with and it was going to be harder to hide if we waltzed in with a just-fucked grin on our faces when the office was full of people.

But as much as I knew we needed to stop, I couldn't speak the word. Feeling myself harden with her on top of me, her tits pressed against my chest, and her body wriggling while she used my cock to try and get friction. I held her still, positioning myself between her legs so when she rocked, she could use the whole length of my cock.

"You trying to get yourself off, baby?" My hands moved to her hips, encouraging her to move. "Using me instead of your hand?"

"Yes." Her eyes flared, her hair falling over her face as she dropped her chin.

"Uh-uh, sweetheart. You want to use me to get off, you have to let me watch you do it."

It seemed only fair.

She lifted her head, tilting her hips as she continued to move. "You know, you could help me?"

The offer was tempting; I'll give her that. But she'd poked fun at my plans for our non-date-dinner and I had a point to prove.

"I could." My hands twitched at her hips. "But I won't."

It was kind of stupid because in reality I was only punishing myself. If she kept going, she was guaranteed to get hers. And instead of joining her, I was resolved to look on like a pervert, and deny myself out of some warped sense of making a point.

Her hips ground into mine, tempting me just to reach out and put us both out of our misery. But for the first time—probably ever—fucking her wasn't the most important thing on my mind.

I leaned toward her and kissed again, taking her mouth like I'd done earlier. She moaned in my mouth, rocking in my lap as my hand tangled in her hair. And I was so close to saying "screw it," that I could have my cake and eat it too when the alarm on my phone sounded.

It wasn't the *wake-up-asshole* one I'd already silenced, but the *you-better-get-your-shit-together-or-you'll-be-late* one I rarely needed.

Cursing myself, and with a pain in my balls that wasn't going to be easily forgotten, I pulled away and grinned. "Need to get into the shower, sweetheart. Last thing I need is to be fired because of my constant lateness. Unless that's your plan?" My brow rose. "Seducing me to insubordination?"

She laughed, her smile lighting up her face as she pushed back on my chest. "No, I hadn't thought of that. But I have to say, it is mighty tempting."

That wasn't the only thing that was tempting.

She let out a yelp as I lifted her off of my lap and gently tossed her to the mattress. "You'll have to try harder than that," I grinned, striding to the shower where I turned the water to artic.

Not that it helped, especially not when she came into the bathroom moments later, sat on the edge of the tub and watched with interest.

A decent man would have showered, got out, toweled off and walked away. But I'd already punished myself once already that morning and I didn't intend to continue.

So, instead of being the decent man we both knew I wasn't, I twisted the faucets so I was no longer in danger of hyperthermia and then let her watch as I jerked off.

Her eyes widened, chewing her bottom lip as she looked on with heated interest. The blush crept up her cheeks as my grip tightened, the strokes getting harder and faster as I brought my-self to the end. It was faster than I would have liked, preferring to make it last longer especially if she was my audience. But we were on the clock, and if the plan had been to be slow and late I would have just fucked her in that bed.

Instead, I came into my palm with a shout, needing my other hand to steady myself against the tile. And then, without saying a fucking word, I finished my shower and shut off the water.

Throwing the towel around my waist, I stepped out of the stall still mostly wet and bent down to kiss her. "I'd love to stay and watch you, beautiful, but one of us has to be responsible."

"I-I'm the responsible one," she stammered, clearly affected by my little show.

"Not today it seems," I chuckled. "But I promise I'll make it up to you tonight *after* I take you to dinner."

"On the not-date-date?" Her eyes struggled to stay on mine, wandering down to droplets of water slithering down my torso. Her tongue darted out and licked her perfect pink lips and I almost came again in the towel.

My head nodded, holding on to the last thread of self-control I had as I took a step toward the bathroom door. "Yep. Now get ready."

I dressed in my bedroom while she showered quickly, then went out to the kitchen to make us both coffee while she got ready. I'd meant what I said about my self-control waning, and didn't trust myself to stay and watch.

When she appeared, she was dressed in the same clothes she had on yesterday—the blouse and skirt, a little worse for wear.

"Can we swing by my apartment and pick something else up?" She looked down at her outfit, not pleased with her appearance. "I can't walk into the office like this."

A glance at my watch told me we didn't have the time but like a sucker, I didn't have it in me to deny her. "Sure, but we have to leave now."

We drove to her apartment in relative silence but there was an ease between us that didn't need words. There was no pressure to fill the void with unnecessary chatter, my body relaxing into the seat as we made the quick trip to where she lived.

"I'll be quick." She popped open the door and leaped onto the sidewalk. "Just circle the block if you need to and I'll be right down."

I reached across, stopping the door from closing and meeting her eye. "Pack a bag while you're at it so we don't have to worry about coming back tomorrow."

She hesitated for a second, and I wasn't sure if she wanted to tell me I was an arrogant prick for assuming or accuse me of bossing her around. But regardless of what words were floating through her head, she didn't say any of them. Instead she nodded, closing the car door and jogging into her apartment building.

True to her word, I only had the circle once before she appeared back on the sidewalk wearing fresh clothes with a small overnight bag on her shoulder. She climbed into the car, a waft of her floral perfume invading the confined space as she shut the door behind her.

"How fast can you drive?" She looked at the digital display on my dashboard and reading the time as almost nine.

"Fasten your seatbelt and you'll find out." I grinned, pulling out into traffic the minute I heard the metallic click of the buckle.

There was no way in hell we were going to make it in time. Not unless my car turned into a rocket ship and levitated above the sea of brake lights. But with a flick of my thumb, I activated my blue-tooth, dialing B&B's reception as she glanced across at me with concern.

"Hello Baldwin and Blake, how may I direct your call?" Martha's sunny voice echoed out of my speakers.

"Martha, it's Kyle. Sarah and I had a meeting with a client and are running a little late. Can you push back our nine o'clock with the art department?"

"Oh, of course, Kyle." Her voice a little cheerier learning who was on the other end of the line. "Anything for you."

Sarah rolled her eyes and I had to stifle the laugh, enjoying her reaction whenever another woman seemed to show interest. "Thanks a lot, Martha. I owe you one." I ended the call and stopped riding the bumper of the car in front of us.

"I'm not sure if I should be worried about your apparent ability to hypnotize every vagina in a fifty-mile radius, or concerned we might get questioned about our mystery meeting." She folded her arms across her chest, looking absently out the windshield.

My hand reached across the console, squeezing her knee. "There's only one vagina I'm interested in hypnotizing. I can't help it if poor Martha finds me charming." I chuckled. "And the meeting—if it comes up—is with Newman Enterprises. An old college friend of mine just got promoted and owes me a favor. I'd already planned to send him a proposal for their next marketing campaign, I'll just do it via email instead of a face-to-face."

"Newman Enterprise?" she asked suspiciously.

"Yes, they're emerging, so not a big fish by any account. But money is money and they're looking to go public next year. We get in on the ground level and we'll be pulling the big bucks when they inevitably explode."

"No." She shook her head. "I meant, you just have something like that in your back pocket? You know, most of us have to work our asses off to get leads. You just seem to have them drop in your lap."

Despite the accusation, it hadn't been animosity that was coating her tone. It was curiosity, which was a change I hadn't expected so soon. I had no doubt she'd heard the bullshit they said about me, the whispers of my prowess in the boardroom. But what every single one of those bastards had failed to mention was that it was hard freaking work and not luck that was responsible for my "good fortune."

"It might look like they land in my lap, but I assure you, it doesn't work that way. There's a lot of stuff that happens behind the scenes; saying the right things, shaking the right hands, reading the right reports. While my friends were off getting blowjobs at the local bar, I was working on getting an internship, learning the market, making connections."

It was refreshing to be honest, to not have to perpetuate the lie. Shit, I couldn't remember a time I hadn't given anyone a straight answer. Usually I just smirked, let them believe whatever they wanted to believe, and went about my business. But with Sarah, I didn't want to do that. Maybe I was getting soft or maybe it was *her* vagina that had hypnotized *me*?

"Oh." She sounded surprised, probably expecting the rote answer that I usually gave. "Well, you make it look easy." She shifted in her seat, looking a little bit embarrassed.

And fuck me if I didn't love seeing her a little unraveled. Proof that she was showing me a side that she didn't usually grandstand either. "Making it look easy is the goal," I chuckled. "It's part of the distraction."

"Ahhhhh, guess I'll have to work on that. Learn how to better conjure up a distraction." She grinned, giving me a knowing smile.

Little did she know she didn't have to do shit. She *was* the distraction. I was positive when men looked at her they saw the beautiful face and the knockout body. But her brain . . . that was far more dazzling than any other part of her.

We arrived at the office a little past nine thirty and I let her go in ahead while I parked the car. It wasn't me just being chivalrous either, I just really liked the sway of her ass when she walked away.

Me, waiting in the car while she walked in, just gave me an excuse to look at it on the company dime.

"How was the meeting?" Kennedy was waiting for me by the elevator when I finally went in. She wore her usual grin, her eyes wide in expectation.

I stepped out of the elevator and strode past her. "It was fine. We'll close on them by next week."

"You'll *close* on them, huh?" She trotted behind me, not done with the conversation. "You don't fool me for a second, Drake."

Normally I would have ignored her statement and moved on. But I knew how much Kennedy meant to Sarah and for some reason, and for the most part she was harmless. After all, she was the one responsible for getting me and Sarah together in that bar. Some might say, I owed her.

"Kennedy." I turned, the bubbly brunette almost barreling into me. "If there's something you need to say, just say it. But if it's about Sarah and I, I'd remind you that now is *not* the time to have that conversation."

She squeaked, taking a step back. "I just meant." Pause. She found some composure before she tried again. "Just don't be an asshole, okay?"

It was endearing that she was watching out for her, but she didn't need to. Not where I was concerned at least.

"I'll do my best." I tried not to grin as I tipped my head to my doorway. "You coming in to warn me off some more or are we done here?"

Her shoulders pushed back as her chin rose. "Nope, we're fine. I've said what I had to say."

"Good. Good chat." And with that I opened my office door,

walked inside and then closed it behind me.

And I had just made it to my desk as my cell lit up with an incoming call.

Keely.

Great.

It seemed like my morning interrogation wasn't done just yet.

14

Sarah

IT WASN'T EASY TO PRETEND like I wasn't attracted to Kyle, but I refused to let everything I'd ever worked for be taken apart by a man. Besides, who knew how long the fascination would last? It had only been a few days and I was in uncharted territory.

All this time I thought I wasn't capable of casual relationships. Guess all it took was the right circumstances. And possibly the right guy, and Kyle was definitely the *right* guy.

Of course Kennedy wanted to know everything, apparently she'd tried to get information from Kyle and was shot down pretty quickly. Not that there were any surprises there, the man was a vault. I had no idea what he was thinking half the time, and the other half, I wasn't sure was the full story. I didn't think he was lying, but there was just something . . . held back about him. It intrigued me, and pulled me in on a level I hadn't experienced before. I just hoped the curiosity and attraction wouldn't be my downfall.

We worked the rest of the day without incident. And true to his word, he didn't lay an improper hand anywhere near me.

I pretended I wasn't disappointed considering it was my own damn rule, going about our business like I wasn't counting down the hours to our non-date-date.

Just another thing that intrigued me.

He said he didn't date, but he wanted to take me out. Was it some weird game? A way to keep me on my toes? Or did he figure we had to eventually eat, especially considering all the sex we were having so it might as well be together?

Kyle Drake was a puzzle I couldn't quite work out, but I was enjoying the challenge.

We left together—considering I hadn't driven in and he was my ride home, it was unavoidable—but miraculously no one seemed to notice. Perhaps it was just me who thought our mutual arrivals and departures looked suspect. Or maybe everyone just figured since we were working together it would make sense working similar hours. After all, I had on more than one occasion arrived at the same time as other co-workers and no one had assumed the worst. I just really needed to get over myself and enjoy the first—and probably only—fling I'd dared participate in.

"Are we going back to your place?" I asked, the car heading north instead of the direction his apartment was in. We were both still dressed in our work clothes and I assumed we would have changed before . . . well before whatever it was that he had planned.

He shook his head, giving nothing away. "No time. You have a burning need to visit my apartment, sweetheart? We both know what will happen if we go there." He didn't even try to hide the smirk.

I rolled my eyes, pretending that it hadn't been on my mind. It had been a long day and I might have been looking forward to a little playtime before dinner. Wasn't that what flings were supposed to do? Binge on sex. Clearly I didn't know the rules.

"Well, will you at least tell me where you are taking me?" My eyes glanced out the window, hoping to find a clue. "Is it dinner? Or something else?"

His lips thinned, hiding his grin. "You'll see when we get there. But if food is on your mind, don't worry, I've got that covered too."

So it was more than dinner?

Damn him and his vault!

Rather than sit there quietly, I instead embarked on a game of twenty questions.

Was it a movie?

Some kind of show?

A museum?

A walk in the park?

Was my current attire appropriate—not that it would make a lick of difference apparently.

But no matter what I asked, it didn't get me any closer to guessing.

For all I knew he was going to charter a private boat on Manhattan Harbor and take me treasure hunting, and seriously, I probably wouldn't have been surprised.

It wasn't until we pulled up to a parking lot that his diabolical plan was revealed.

Oh. Hell. No.

"You can't be serious." I looked at the brightly flashing neon that welcomed us. "Bowling? You're taking me bowling?"

Not sure if it was surprise or panic that I felt, but I could feel my heart racing and not in a good way.

Kyle let out a throaty laugh clearly expecting my exact reaction. "Sure, why not? We're both competitive, figured we'd take it out on the lanes."

"Pick something else," I demanded. "Anything else. We can go throw darts? Or shoot pool? Or even tennis, I'm positive there's a court that has evening sessions." I didn't even care I wasn't dressed for tennis, it was infinitely better than the alternative.

"So what is concerning you the most? Having to wear someone else's shoes? Or the fact the place looks like it needs a flea bath?" His head tilted to the side, reading my mind exactly.

I didn't hesitate, shaking my head as my fingers knotted into an anxious ball in my lap. "All of it. It's just not me. Can't we do something else?"

"It's just not you, huh?" He seemed genuinely surprised. "You mean the *you* who works at Baldwin and Blake and has her files alphabetized and color coded? Or the *you* who married a complete stranger a few months ago? Because Vegas Sarah—the woman I married—was up for anything."

"Yeah well, that was when I thought I wasn't going to see you again. It was easy to pretend to be someone else." I shook off his taunt.

"Don't." His hand moved to my lap, covering my still knotted fingers. "Don't pretend that the version I met wasn't as real as the version I'm looking at today. I get you like to compartmentalize. I get you like order, and structured plans, and clean bars with fancy cocktail glasses. But there's another side of you, a side that by some miracle you let someone else see. And I'm not going to let you shove her back in the box and forget she existed."

His response floored me, as was the look he was giving me, peering through the bullshit. "It's just difficult for me, I like—"

"Yes, but you can like other things too." His hand moved to

my chin, his fingers tracing my jaw. "Let's just try, okay? Pretend you're never going to see me or any of these people again. And if you hate it, I'll take you to a swanky five-star restaurant with starched napkins and shiny cutlery."

My fists tightened, the words to tell him I didn't want to stuck in my throat as his fingers continued to caress me. It felt so nice; the barest of touches on my skin sending a zap of lightening up my spine.

"Fine, but if I hate it, we go," I shot back indignantly, pretending I was annoyed. But it wasn't anger I was feeling, it was fear—pushing myself out of my comfort zone, which seemed to be a theme when he was around.

He grinned, reveling that he'd gotten his way. "Promise. And I'll even let you write up the scoreboard, I'll play under any name you like."

Well, the prospect of naming him *Asshat* for the evening was tempting, after all, he did say any name. But even before I had a chance to agree, my seatbelt unbuckled, sliding across my chest like magic.

We both exited the car, his arm finding its way around my waist. I guess we were no longer at work so the no touching rule didn't apply, and damn if he wasn't making the most of it.

His hand dropped to my ass, giving it a squeeze as we approached the counter, paid for a couple of games and got our—help me lord—bowling shoes. And thankfully, they also sold sports socks, a pair added to our total before we checked out. I didn't care I hadn't gotten a chance to launder them yet, or the fact I looked ridiculous with a bright pair of white crew socks and my pencil skirt. I'd take humiliation over a fungal infection any day of the week.

Kyle didn't even hide the fact he was checking me out as I sat down and put on my shoes, his eyes glued to the front of my blouse as I bent to tie up the laces.

"Um hello?" I waved a hand, calling him on his obvious gawking. "Eyes up here, buddy."

His lips spread into a grin with zero apology. "I figured I was going to be spending most of the night staring at your ass when tossing the ball down the lane, I didn't want them to feel left out."

I shook my head, completely unsurprised he would take what was supposed to be a wholesome activity and make it dirty. Hell, he could be at a church bake sale and find some innuendo somewhere. "Behave, *Asshat*." Using his new moniker as I pointed at him with accusation. "I'm wearing someone else's shoes and a pair of gym socks I haven't washed yet. You can at least pretend not to be enjoying this whole exercise."

"Asshat, huh?" He shrugged, pulling on his own shoes. "And for the record, I am enjoying every minute of this and I have no interest in pretending I'm not."

I scoffed, ignoring him as I went to the touch screen and entered our names. Him, Asshat, as planned. And for me, just plain Sarah. My finger was just about to lock us in when his hand stopped me. "And I get to pick the name for you."

"That wasn't the deal."

"We never decided on who picked your name, I only agreed you could pick mine."

Gah, he was right.

Doing what he always did and finding some—no matter how obscure it was—loophole and getting his own way.

I could have argued, but to be honest, I didn't really care. It was a stupid name on a board that no one would ever see. And did it really matter what he wrote? He could call me Ms. Asshat or something equally as unflattering, and it still wouldn't bother me. For some reason, it just didn't.

Sigh.

"Fine, write my name." I moved my hand from the button, allowing him to delete the letters of my name and tap in some of his own.

My eyes watching his finger as he spelled out "Sweet Cheeks."

"What?" I turned to him, pointing at the overhead screen that proudly displayed our duo of Asshat and Sweet Cheeks.

"Just keeping with the theme, darling. And your ass is most definitely sweet." He winked, moving to the rack of balls and selecting one.

He chose a blue one, weighing it in his hand before carrying it back. "This one is for you, it's a little on the heavy side but trust me, you can handle it."

It was strange how easily the compliment rolled off his tongue. Most guys would have handed me a lighter ball, assuming I was weak, but Kyle saw something else.

Before I had a chance to thank him, he went to retrieve a ball for himself, returning and gesturing it was my turn to go first.

"I-I." I wiggled my fingers into the holes. "I'm really bad at this."

I didn't bowl.

The last time I *did* bowl was one time in middle school. And I'm pretty sure I managed to weasel out of my turn when it came around.

"Is this your way of trying to seduce me, Sarah?" He lowered his ball and put his arms around my waist. "Throw me off my game? Not saying I don't approve of your tactics, but you'll have to try a little harder than that."

My head shook, rolling my eyes as I sighed. "I'm not trying to seduce you. And if I were, there would be a different set of balls in my hands."

He laughed, the chuckle bubbling up his throat as his body shook against me. "Now, you're talking. But let's wait until we get back to my apartment. This might not be the nicest of establishments but fairly sure public indecency would be frowned upon."

His hands moved up my back and settled on my shoulders. "Just relax, Sarah. Roll it down the middle and see how it spins. You won't know how to do it until you actually try."

Well, wasn't that the truth. Some people got their guidance from the pulpit, I got mine from a dingy bowling alley from my fake husband. Guess it kept things interesting.

Taking a breath, I relaxed my body as instructed and felt Kyle's hands pull away. Then with as much grace—my pencil skirt restricting my movement—as I could manage, I tossed the ball down the center lane.

Or at least that was what I had attempted to do, the blue ball of wonder hitting the side and rolling down the gutter.

Kyle chuckled, putting his arms around me and kissing the back of my neck. "Technique wasn't bad, we just need to work on your aim."

Of course next it was his turn, he knocked eight of the pins out and picked up the last couple on the spare. But to his credit, he didn't brag, instead deciding it was time to order our *fancy* dinner of hotdogs, fries and beer.

Honestly, while it was not a date—non-date or regular—I would have chosen in a million years, it was kind of nice.

I did manage to get some points on the board, more from blind luck than any athletic talent. But there were no surprises as to who won, Kyle deliberately threw a game or two so it wasn't an outright slaughter. And when it was over— the fast food and games done—I was surprised at how much I'd enjoyed myself. I hadn't thought about the dingy interior, and what germs were probably crawling on those bench seats. I hadn't thought about the processed food I tried to avoid especially during the week. And the fact I was wearing borrowed shoes that looked ridiculous had faded from importance as well. It was like I'd been inoculated, immune to the niggling bad thoughts that usually plagued my mind.

"You ready to go, gorgeous?" Kyle handed our rented shoes back and put his arm around my waist.

Without hesitation I nuzzled into his side. "Yeah, take me to your apartment, Kyle."

15

Kyle

SLEEPING WITH SARAH NEVER GOT old.

Especially not since she left her bullshit-buttoned-up attitude at the door. I'd always known she was a wildcat, and she was proving day after day that the fire inside of her wasn't just reserved for the boardroom. And wasn't it a fucking treat that I got to see both. Watching her absolutely dominate in the office, and then scream my name underneath me as she lost control.

And that's how it was for us.

Work.

Sex.

Wash.

Rinse.

Repeat.

It wasn't all just fucking though, with my interest in her extending beyond ways to make her come. I found out she'd always wanted to travel but had decided her career meant more to her. I suggested hopping a plane and heading to Paris for the weekend, but she'd assumed I'd been joking. What she didn't know was if she'd said yes, she would have been eating crepes instead of bagels.

She got under my skin, into my pores, and I liked spending time with her. And while I had no idea what the situation had morphed into, I had zero interest in trying to define it. Instead, we danced our little tango around it, leaving it for a conversation I was happy not to have.

Keely was another fucking matter. And I thanked every single mile between us and the child she was incubating stopping her from getting on a plane. Every day there was a new barrage of text and voice messages demanding to meet Sarah, my new "wife." And it was Sarah who eventually convinced me to put her out of her misery and confirm that we weren't actually married. She knew we'd met in Vegas and I was seeing her, but as much as I loved my sister, she was informed that my love life was out of bounds. I didn't expect for her to listen, but figured it would give me at least another week or two before I got the third degree.

If there was any doubt that Kennedy had been given a full debrief, it was put to rest about a week later. She was more skittish than usual and while she hadn't come to my office and given me any more thinly veiled threats, she didn't extend anymore offers of being *friendly* either. It seemed she'd deferred her role as ambassador to Sarah, and any further invitations of work related drinks were strictly curated by her.

"You compile those files for Barnes and Yarrow?" She strolled in looking like a corporate wet dream, red lips twitching with intent while her pencil skirt did its best to look demure. Pity I knew better.

"And if I say no?" I lifted my brow, arching back into my office chair and admiring the view. It was something I was positive I'd never get sick of, and not just because she was beautiful. That smart mouth and fierce eyes never failed to get me hard.

Her eyes narrowed, not cutting me any slack even though I'd made her come three times before we'd started our day. "Then I'll tie you to that chair until they're done." She said it with a smile, but I had no doubt she'd follow through.

I laughed, unable to help myself. "If that was meant as a punishment, you fell short. Not that I've ever let a woman tie me to a chair, but I'd be happy to let you be the first."

The door was open which is why I kept my voice low, but there was no denying she'd heard me, the heat simmering in her eyes as she walked closer.

"Not here," she warned, glancing out to the hall before closing the door. "But I'm not averse to tying you up, Kyle. In fact, it *is* something I'd like to try."

And didn't that get my attention. My sweet little innocent—or so everyone thought—Sarah telling me exactly what she wanted without so much as a stutter. No blushing either, just a cheeky smile that could keep me hard for a week.

My eyes cut to the door, and I cursed every single one of those bastards outside of it. I didn't care they had nothing to do with it, or the hours I had left before I could touch her. I was pissed beyond measure that the most perfect woman in the world was standing right in front of me and I had to sit on my hands like an asshole.

I stood slowly, watching as her eyes flared as she took in what I had to offer. We'd had a strict no-fucking-around-at-work policy up until that point but judging by the way she was licking her lips, I wasn't the only one reconsidering it.

"Anything else you want to try, sweetheart?" Because I'd be more than happy to help her explore whatever fantasies she had. Hell, I'd tick them off one by one like it was my own personal mission.

There was no denying we both felt it, that crackle in the air between us. She wanted me as much as I wanted her and there was only a thread of self-control saving us from tearing each other's clothes off and acting like savages.

"Hey, Sarah, you in there?" The knock at the door broke the moment, Kennedy's cheery voice ensuring that whatever plans we had were put back on ice. "Caleb is asking about that Barnes and Yarrow file, he has a meeting this afternoon."

Sarah bit her lip, her brow scrunching in apology as she turned back to the door and opened it. "Hey, we were just working on it."

No we fucking weren't, but pointing that out served no purpose.

Kennedy wasn't an idiot, something I was further reminded of when her eyes floated between Sarah and I. We might have been standing a respectable distance apart, both still wearing our clothes, but it was clear she'd interrupted something.

"Sorry, didn't realize you guys were in a *meeting*." She used air quotes, raising her eyebrows in case her intonation wasn't enough.

Sarah laughed nervously, that confident woman who'd told me she wanted to tie me to a chair missing in action as she shrugged. "No, we were just discussing the client. I'll be out in a second."

I hated that.

That Sarah still felt the need to censor herself even for someone who was supposed to be her best friend. Not that I'd expected her to confess that we'd been seconds away from defiling my desk, but she could have done better than that bullshit excuse.

Kennedy nodded, mouthing a sarcastic "okay" before leaning against the doorjamb. "Well, when you're both done *discussing*, you might want to hand in those files to your boss. Unless you want him to come down here and ask for them himself."

"Thanks Kennedy, we've got it from here." Sarah's voice

hardened, not giving her a chance to respond before closing the door.

It was tempting to say something, ask her why she hadn't just told Kennedy to mind her own business. But she got enough pressure from everyone else so she wasn't going to get that kind of grief from me.

"Here." I reached onto my desk and handed her the report I'd been working on. "Barnes and Yarrow."

I watched as her fingers wrapped around the papers, giving them a tug as I refused to let them go. "We'll continue this conversation later when we don't have to worry about interruptions."

She smirked, keeping her eyes locked on mine. "I was counting on it."

Against my better judgment I let go, the file she'd been so intent on getting no longer in my possession as she pressed it against her chest.

Mmmmmm. Nice.

"Get out of here before I change my mind," I chuckled, turning back to my desk. "Or it will be me who's doing the tying up."

I didn't need to see her face to know she was probably excited, the subtle noise of fabric shifting more than a clue she was probably pressing her thighs together on that thought alone. And yeah, it fucking pleased me. Because clearly we both got off on a little delayed gratification.

But that delay only lasted until she was in my apartment, or I was in hers, and then all bets were off. But ironically it wasn't just for sex, Sarah's prone body warm against mine as she slept, the perfect description of heaven.

I loved everything about her, from the curve of her ass to

the smell of her shampoo, but most of all I loved the unrelenting fierceness of her eyes and the amazing sound of her laugh. She was both a disease and the cure, and I wanted her more than was wise. But it wasn't until Friday that I found out exactly how unwise those feelings were.

I was about to drive Sarah home, when Kennedy pried open the elevator door, crashing our ride down to the underground garage.

"Damn, you guys are quick. I didn't think I was going to make it." She grabbed her chest dramatically, her breath heaving like she'd just run a sprint.

"Not quick enough." I rolled my eyes, earning me an elbow to the ribs from Sarah.

"Ignore him, was there something you needed?" She turned giving her friend her attention.

It wasn't snide or angry, and but then Sarah rarely got that way with people she cared about. It was endearing and curious, something I was seeing more and more of as the time passed.

Kennedy dropped her award-winning performance and straightened, smirking as she hugged Sarah. "You, silly. I've missed you and it's been a few weeks."

There was a subtext to the conversation that clearly I'd missed, Sarah's hand flying up to her mouth as she hugged Kennedy back. "Shit, I'm sorry. I've been a really bad friend."

"And why is that?"

Yeah, probably could have kept my mouth shut because none of it concerned me. But I wasn't exactly good with doing what I should, and hearing Sarah say she was anything other than fucking perfect annoyed the shit out of me.

"I've been busy—" Sarah started before she was cut off.

"Well, before you guys had this *thing* happening." Kennedy punctuated with air quotes. "Sarah and I would always go out on a Friday. We'd drink, and talk girl stuff, and I've let the last few weeks slide because . . ." She waved her hands gesturing to me. "Well, I'm not trying to get in the way of my girl getting some."

"Oh really?" My curiosity was peaked, wondering what else would happen on these little Friday night excursions. Sarah didn't do casual hook-ups, so I doubted men were in her equation. Not that I thought it stopped any of those cocksuckers from trying. It made me irrationally irritated.

"It was just a way to let the steam off after the week." Sarah shrugged, down playing it like it was no big deal. "A little bit of fun."

Yeah, I was well aware how much *fun* it was seeing her relaxed after a few drinks on the dance floor. I'd been treated to that when we first met, and not sure I wanted to share.

"Every. Friday. Night," Kennedy annunciated. "The two of us. No significant others allowed. And I think it's time I got my wingman back. Just so you know."

It was clear that I was the *you* in question.

"Sarah can do what she likes, when she likes, and with who she likes," I fired back, a little annoyed that Kennedy felt she needed to speak for Sarah. "She doesn't need anyone's permission."

The woman I was spending my days and my nights with was more than capable of speaking for herself, and I wished the people around her would see her in the same light. I wasn't sure what pissed me off more, Kennedy trying to invoke girl code and "reserve" her for the evening, or the fact she assumed I was keeping her sequestered.

"Really?" Kennedy asked, leaning in a little closer. "You're not going to get all caveman jealous if she happens to talk or dance with some other guy?"

I'd obviously not given much thought about the statement until after it had come out of my mouth. Because I was *very* particular about whom she did certain things with. Yep, not my finest moment, and not something I intended to repeat either. But dragging her back to my place by the hair wasn't a good plan either considering I'd just made a big deal about her not needing anyone else's opinion.

My jaw was clenched, but I managed to get the words out without strangling them. "If that's what she wants to do, then that's what she'll do."

Of all the bullshit I'd said in recent times, that had to take the cake. Because yes, I fucking cared and the chance of me going *caveman* were high if I saw another man even breathe in her direction.

"Ok-ay." Kennedy tapped her foot awkwardly as the elevator opened to the garage. "Looks like we're set for tonight then. Great."

Yeah, fucking great.

"Can you give us a minute?" Sarah turned to Kennedy as she stepped out. "I'll get a ride home with Kyle and meet you back at my place."

"Sure." Kennedy shrugged. "Don't punk out on me though, all right?"

"I won't." Sarah smiled and watched as Kennedy hit the keyless entry to her blue Mazda hatch and climbed inside.

Heat prickled at my neck, the mood noticeably cooler than when we'd left the office.

"So you think I should see other people?" She didn't give me a chance to start. "I wasn't really sure how this was going to work."

"That's not what I said, and not what I meant."

We waited until Kennedy drove off before continuing.

"I meant generally you should do what you want." I was careful with my word choice; I wanted to be clear without sounding like a complete asshole. "This week I've seen you go toe to toe with CEOs and not bat an eye. You're fearless, and you sure as shit don't need to ask permission."

"So are you going to see other people?" she asked, the little line at the bridge of her nose crinkling like it did when she was deep in thought.

"No. I'm not. And I don't want you to either."

I didn't want there to be any other interpretation. While I happily celebrated the version of herself that was more assertive, I wasn't willing to share her with anyone else either.

"But you just said I didn't need to ask permission. And you don't usually date anyway, so . . ."

"Things change." And it wasn't a point I could see myself conceding on.

The parking garage wasn't an ideal place for a discussion—too many eyes and ears—so I tipped my head to my Audi, which at least gave us some privacy.

"I'll drive you home, let's talk in the car."

"Yeah, we should definitely talk."

16

Sarah

I WAS A PLANNER.

I always had been.

So, how I ended up in an undefined relationship with a man I was supposed to be destroying was beyond me.

It was a catastrophe.

Sure, I could pretend like this had been my *plan* all along. Sleep with the enemy, find his weakness and then use whatever it was to destroy him. But it would be complete bullshit to assume my head had any input into this decision.

No. I slept with him because he basically got me wetter than any man and or machine had ever got me before and I couldn't say no. It was primal, an urge that, for the first time in my life, told my brain to "sit the hell down and chill the hell out" and let my hormones take the wheel.

Which they had.

Which was why I was sleeping with a man I was technically not dating, who I was working with, and who I was supposed to hate.

And then my feelings got involved. And I wasn't even sure it was just sex anymore. Because maybe if it were, I'd forgive myself.

But noooooooooo, clearly I couldn't just let myself have hot sex with the guy, I had to become invested. Actually really like the guy even though he made it clear he wasn't interested in relationships and would probably break my stupid heart.

Not to mention it could totally screw my career, which had been the reason why I'd wanted to destroy him in the first place. So unless I wanted to be handed a cardboard box to pack up my coffee cup and picture frames along with my marching orders in a few months, I was not acting smart.

All my excellent and careful prior planning didn't count for shit.

I was a moron.

Shit.

My eyes darted across to him, his hands locked on the steering wheel as we exited the garage and onto the street.

"Sooooooo." What the hell did I want or even need to say?

"You want to fuck other people?" he asked. Unlike me, not having any problems at all articulating *his* feelings.

"No." I choked back a laugh. Me, the serial relationship-er have more than one casual whatever this was? "I mean, you know that I suck at random . . ."

"*Fucking.*" That word against those lips was positively obscene. "I've heard you say the word before, and it's a favorite of mine. You should say it more often."

"I have no problem saying *fuck* when necessary." I rolled my eyes. Sure, I didn't pepper my conversation with it, but I wasn't averse to swearing.

"Fuck," he glanced over to me, "is always necessary."

See how easy it was to tumble down the rabbit hole? He started talking like that, looking like that and I forgot everything and started wondering why I wasn't undressing already.

"No, I don't want to fuck other people," I shot back, still mostly confused.

"Good." He nodded, his smile spreading across his lips. "Just me then."

"Well, I should probably stop that too," I heard myself say, the words surprising me.

"No. You shouldn't," he answered casually, keeping his eyes on the road.

"Look, it's obvious I'm attracted to you." Considering it had only taken me twenty-four hours from vowing to ruin him to jumping into bed with him, I think that was stating the obvious. "But my job is the most important thing to me right now. I don't want to do anything that will jeopardize it. And if Caleb and Adele found out we are—"

"Fucking," he added before I could finish.

"Fucking," I repeated. "Then I'm almost positive one of us, if not both of us, would lose our jobs."

We'd been careless, and I was already making stupid decisions—like having feelings for someone who was supposed to be a fling—I couldn't risk the one thing I had that made sense in my life. The one thing I was good at.

"I disagree." He shook his head. "B&B's fraternization policy specifies only relationships where either party is in the chain of command that it becomes a problem. We're exempt by that definition."

"You know the fraternization policy?"

I wasn't sure if I was impressed or horrified. And don't even get me started on the fact that part of me was secretly thrilled it wouldn't be something I'd lose my job over. No. Horrified. Be horrified, I tried to tell myself. Who even does that?

"Don't be so surprised." He laughed, his coolness rolling off in a wave of self-assurance. "I assumed you knew the policy too, considering your attention to detail."

See, evidence right there that I had dropped the ball.

He turned to look at me, those green eyes of his boring into mine. "I wouldn't have laid a finger on you—or *in* you as the case may be—if I thought there was a chance it would get us fired."

"It's still a bad idea. And you're right, I should have known that and the fact I didn't proves what a distraction this is. It was fun, and sex with you is probably the best I have ever had. But we both know this has no future considering how different we are. Honestly, it was stupid to even start."

My thoughts came out in a rush.

It had been incredibly stupid. Yes, working alongside him had been outstanding, and going to bed with him was an excitement I'd never experienced before. But it wasn't who I was and it wasn't who he was, and the last thing I needed was to throw away the only thing that worked in my life. My job.

"I told you. Things change," he responded calmly. "Obviously I don't have the time or the interest in seeing someone else. It's been a while, but I know how these things work. So, why don't we wait and see what happens between the two of us before you assume the worst-case scenario."

My heart was in my throat, trying to sift through his words and trying to not project my own hopes and dreams like I usually did. What did that even mean?

If he was suggesting we attempt a regular boyfriend/girlfriend relationship then that was the most vague attempt at commitment I'd ever heard.

I didn't do maybes.

I needed a plan.

That was the way I worked. The only way I could operate, and he knew that. The idea of just seeing how it all *worked out* was terrifying, more so because I knew if it all came crashing down, he'd shrug it off and keep going. I wasn't built that way, didn't have the capacity to roll the dice when it came to things that were important. And I'd already flown by the seat of my pants more than I had ever done in my life.

I couldn't hang my hopes on a possibility.

I wouldn't do that.

"I need to concentrate on my job. And the promotion. And prove that I deserve to be there. Not waste time on sex with a man I know I have zero future with." The words were harsher than I'd intended them to be, rushing out before I had a chance to soften them.

Clearly my mouth had said exactly what I'd been thinking. Because as much as I loved being with him, I knew deep down we were too different. And maybe part of me doubted I was enough to keep him interested, the inevitable boredom setting in for him once the chase was done.

No, there wasn't any *real* future for us.

Not one that made sense.

My fists balled in my lap and I wasn't sure which part of myself I was angry at. My head or my heart—because one of them had let me down. Not him though; he'd been the only honest thing in the whole equation and he hadn't deserved my bitchiness even if it was self-preservation.

He was quiet.

Too quiet.

I had basically told him he was a waste of my time and I was no longer interested, and he didn't say a word.

"I'm sorry," I said quickly, knowing it didn't make a difference.

I hated the way it felt, the heaviness between us and knowing I'd caused it. And the longer he went without saying something just made it worse, reminding me how horrible I'd been and how much better he deserved. I wished he would lash out. Call me a bitch, or a whore, or a cock tease. Anything would have been better than the silence.

"Well, that changes things," he finally said, his tone so devoid of emotion it scared me. "Like you said, it was fun, but there's no point continuing if you feel you're *wasting your time.*"

Ok, so maybe it wasn't completely devoid of emotion, the bite in his voice crystal clear. But the truth was I deserved a lot worse than that.

He'd have been totally justified to toss back some of his own barbs, but he didn't. Instead we drove the rest of the way in silence, his hands locked around the steering wheel and not a bad word about me or what I'd done escaping his lips. I wasn't really sure what to say and I had no idea what was going on in his head but it couldn't have been good. And really, if he'd been less decent he might have pulled over to the curb and told me to get out. But he didn't, and deep down I wasn't surprised.

He was a good person, kind and generous and I'd seen that from the moment I'd laid eyes on him in Vegas. And other than an inaccurate job description, he'd never lied to me. Not once, which was more than I could say for most of the men I'd been with.

Maybe under different circumstances this might have worked out. Circumstances where we weren't competing for the same job, or where we were both on the same page as far as relationships. Hell, I didn't even know if he wanted to be in one, or had just said he'd try in order to appease me. And the fact I didn't know was exactly the reason it had to end.

We were too different.

And I wasn't sure I could do different.

His car stopped at the front of my apartment building, the engine continued to idle as I opened my door.

"I'm sorry." I forced myself to look at him, determined I owed him at least that.

"No. Do not apologize." He shook his head, his eyes completely devoid of the anger or irritation I was sure I deserved. "What I said before still stands. You are an incredible and strong woman. Do not ask for permission and don't say sorry if you are doing what you want."

Call me a bitch, please internally I begged, the kindness harder to take.

"Are you sure this is what you want?" His hand reached over and thumbed my lip and I struggled not to lean into it.

My skin craved the contact, wanting to take what I'd said back and accept what he was willing to give. Even though I knew eventually I'd have to give him up, maybe I could keep him a little longer.

No. That wasn't fair, not to either of us and one thing I refused to be was indecisive. I'd made my decision, and I needed to stick to it, no matter how hard it was not to kiss him as he looked at me with those gorgeous eyes of his.

"Yes. It is." I tried to put as much confidence as I could behind it even though part of me was having second thoughts, keeping my balled fists in my lap so I wouldn't touch him.

"Okay, then. I'll see you next week." His voice was dry as he dropped his hand and returned it to the steering wheel.

"Okay." I nodded, unsure if I should say something more even though I had no idea what to say.

It felt unfinished and yet so final.

And unlike other relationships that ended, I was still going to have to see him at work.

"It's not going to be weird on Monday," he said suddenly, as if reading my thoughts. "We were able to segregate this before, so it won't change now. Work is work. Things aren't going to change between us, not there."

If it had been anyone else, I'd have struggled to believe it. But Kyle was different, and I trusted him—and if he said things weren't going to change, then they wouldn't. No one would blame him if he wanted to make it awkward, but he was clearly a more decent human being than most. And if he could do that, then it wouldn't be me who let down the team.

"Thank you." My heart swelled with gratitude, the urge to cry almost overwhelming. "You have been . . . really wonderful."

It was utterly ridiculous that I'd summed up everything he was by simply calling him wonderful. He'd been so much more. But opening my mouth and saying anything else was too risky. He didn't need my gratitude, and anything more was just going to feel condescending.

"Don't mention it." He shrugged, seeming unaffected and even managing to give me a smile. "You should get going, Kennedy will be waiting."

For a second I hesitated, wanting to kiss him. Maybe because I knew that after this it would no longer be acceptable and I would miss it. I'd miss his lips on my skin and his arms around me, the warmth I felt when he was around. I wanted to bottle it up and keep it close, and let it linger just a while longer. But I couldn't, because it wouldn't be fair to send mixed messages even if I was dying to kiss those lips of his one last time.

What I felt couldn't be love. Because how could it be? It was too soon to feel anything like that. But there was something there, more than just friendship or gratitude or even sexual attraction. It was bubbling underneath the surface, an emotion I just couldn't put my finger on, making my heart ache.

I pushed myself out of the car before I changed my mind, forcing myself to look him in the eyes. Even though every cell in my body screamed not to leave, I knew it was the right thing to do. And even though I hadn't wanted to, my mouth followed the script and managed to open, and gave him the "goodbye."

He leaned across the seat, looking at me as I stood on the curb with his mouth pressed into a hard line like he was hesitating. But he didn't say anything, just nodded and told me he'd see me Monday, and then he watched as I walked away.

It was done.

We were done.

17

Kyle

I'D NEVER MISSED A WOMAN.

Not one in particular.

There wasn't time.

Women walked in and out of my life with as much regularity as I allowed. If I liked one, she'd usually stay awhile. And if she didn't, then I'd move on to another. It was great while it lasted but I hadn't found one who made me mourn the loss.

That didn't mean I didn't know what love was.

I was incredibly close to my family. The folks were both gone, both of them dying younger than they should. It wasn't anything tragic or noteworthy like a plane crash. Nope, they just didn't take care of themselves, my dad dying of a stroke and my mother following soon after due to heart disease. But though their lifestyle sucked—the bad diet and lack of exercise a huge contributor to why they were no longer around—they were good parents. Keely and I loved them fiercely, and there was never a question that they didn't feel the same way.

So my apathy to being *in love* wasn't about not getting hugged enough as a child.

The past hadn't just been a string of one-night stands either. When I was with a woman, I was there, engaged. And sure, there were times when I experienced genuine affection toward them. I cared about their wellbeing, I enjoyed seeing them smile and liked them being happy. They weren't just a receptacle for my cock. Okay, maybe some were, but they were more than fine with it, I assure you.

But Sarah was different.

Not sure why, but she was. I was hoping that time would have worked it out for me, test if it was her intelligence or her drive that made the difference. Or if it was her honesty. Maybe it was the combination.

Of course, she was beautiful. And her curves were hard to ignore, but those things weren't what held my attention. Which was exactly what other women hadn't managed to do.

Man, I was pissed.

I might have pretended I didn't give a shit, but I wasn't "all good" with the situation. Not by a long shot.

I went back to my apartment and ordered in and then spent some time being annoyed I was still thinking about it. About her.

Scotch seemed to help for a while and then it started to make things worse. I remembered she and Kennedy—that girl had a lot to answer for—had their standing Friday night *thing*.

I thought about her in a bar, men looking at her and wanting to touch her.

To kiss her.

To. Fuck. Her.

It was irrational to be jealous. That I felt I'd lost her when she'd never really been mine. But there I was anyway, up to my neck in it.

"Keely." I was a little less than sober when I made the call but I figured if anyone was going to get drunk dialed, she was my safest option. "How is my favorite sister?"

"I'm your only sister, Kyle and you sound like you're drinking." She sounded concerned.

"It's a Friday and I've had a little scotch, don't be so dramatic." It's not like I was roaming the streets in a bathrobe for Christ's sake. "Just unwinding after a long week."

"What's wrong? Did something happen at work? Where's Sarah, is she there with you?" She'd started with the rapid-fire questions earlier than usual.

"Yeah, that didn't work out." I laughed, taking a mouthful of what was left in my glass. "I'm a waste of time it seems."

Seriously, when did I turn into such a pussy?

Licking my wounds like some asshole.

It was pathetic and not like me at all.

"What are you talking about? You sound weird." It seemed my sister shared the same sentiment.

"Nothing, forget it. Obviously it's the scotch talking." I tilted the empty glass and inspected it, deciding on whether to have another. "Long story short, she was looking for something else and I wasn't it. It's fine."

"That's ridiculous, you are amazing. She would be lucky to have you. You're smart and hardworking and funny. And you drive a pretentious fast car and dress nice. And as much as I hate to admit it, you aren't ugly."

"Wow, sis. I might tear up." I coughed, pretending to be emotional.

"Stop it, you know you're good looking. Maybe I should talk to her?"

I wasn't sure if she was serious—on second thought, it was my sister who meddled way too much in everyone's lives, she *was* serious—but she wasn't speaking to Sarah.

No one fought my battles, and I didn't need my younger sister singing my praises either. I'd rather just hand her my balls in a box with a nice ribbon around it.

"Yeah, that's not going to happen." That's all I fucking needed, to lose whatever self-respect I had left. Or worse, have her agree to be with me out of fucking sympathy. Maybe calling Keely wasn't such a good idea after all.

"So, obviously you *like* her or you wouldn't be upset."

Yep, definitely a bad idea.

"Who says I'm upset?" I answered drily, annoyed I'd been such an easy read.

"You're drinking alone. On a Friday night. You think I didn't know about the parade of whores who you usually entertain?"

"A little judgmental aren't you?" I laughed. "They were very lovely women, not one of them was a—"

"Whores," she snapped, not allowing me to finish. "Like my dear brother. Oh, yeah. I love you but you were totally a whore too. Why do you think I kept pushing for you to find a girlfriend? I didn't want any of my future children to have to learn a new aunt's name every holiday."

See what I mean? Drama.

Besides, I'd never brought a woman home and I sure as hell wasn't going to start now. Especially considering I seemed to have misplaced my testicles, and the idea of being with another woman made me physically ill.

"Well, we don't have to worry about that now, do we?"

Yeah. I needed to stop drinking.

"You know, you could fight for her. Show her what she obviously means to you. And don't tell me," she added before I had a chance to stop her. "That it's not worth it or some other bullshit you are going to use as an excuse. I bet you haven't even told her why you moved to New York."

"She knows I'm here for the experience. Climb the corporate ladder." I gave her the usual rote response. "Choose some other valid reason here."

"Except for the real one," she fired back. "Because if any of those reasons were true, you would have stayed at Stockwell and been the youngest partner in their history."

"Don't," I warned.

That conversation with me was volatile at best. Add in the booze and my clouded judgment and it was not something I wanted to revisit.

"Don't what?" She didn't back down. "Care about my brother? Be concerned about his happiness? Be proud that he walked away from large amounts of money and career prospects because he has loyalty and cares about his sister? Choose *your* valid reason here."

She was more like me than I thought. And smart too. Add in sarcastic for good measure and as much as I wanted to, there was no way I could stay angry at her. Besides, she'd been through enough.

"I should have ruined them." I gripped the phone so tight in my hand I heard the plastic casing crack. "I should have—"

"No, you promised." Her voice softened. "And I'm happy, really I am. And I don't want any more people getting hurt because of me."

I hated that she thought it, that she felt any of it was her fault.

"None of this was because of you, don't you dare take responsibility."

"Kyle, stop," she said with so much authority it actually made my head snap. "Tell her. Let her see the *real* you."

God, I was proud of her.

She could be a pain in the ass sometimes, but fuck, she was amazing. And she had more compassion in her little finger than I had in my entire body. But there was no way I was going down that road with Sarah. It wouldn't happen.

"If I have to convince someone just to date me, sis, there's really not much point. I love you. I'm always going to love you. But you don't always know what's best for me."

I was done and so was the conversation. And shit was going to be fine because I said it was going to be. And there would be plenty more fish in the sea blah, blah, blah.

"I love you, Kyle." It killed me there was sadness in her voice. "Don't sleep with any more whores."

"Night, kiddo," I chuckled.

I'd give myself one night to be a miserable asshole.

One night to piss and moan and feel sorry for myself. But after that I was moving the fuck on. Not by sleeping with another woman, because we already established I probably couldn't get hard if I tried. But doing what Sarah seemed so hell bent on. Business. If I couldn't sleep with her and have her in my personal life then we were going to be the best senior marketing executives Baldwin & Blake had ever seen. And clearly I was a sad sack because seeing her happy was more fucking important than dating her.

Great.

Awesome.

God, this was *not* going to be fun.

18

IT HAD BEEN EXACTLY FOUR weeks since I stopped sleeping with Kyle.

Four weeks and three days to be exact. I also knew the hours and the minutes, but even thinking them to myself sounded pathetic so I pretended I didn't know and that I didn't care. They were the lies I told myself, along with me being fine with the way things were.

Kyle had promised it wouldn't be weird and surprisingly, it wasn't. I'm not sure what sorcery he performed or if he'd made special offerings to the corporate gods, but when we walked in on that first Monday morning it was business as usual.

He wasn't cold to me, or rude or even—and what would totally be justified—distant. He smiled, made sure he always made eye contact and was respectful whenever we spoke, which was a lot. There was no avoiding, no snide remarks, no animosity of any kind.

He was completely hands off—not touching me in any way except for a few cursory nudges whenever we sat too close at a meeting. And most of all, he didn't flirt. Not even a little.

For me, it was a little harder to switch off.

Even though it had been me who had called time-out, I found

myself looking at him sometimes and remembering how his lips felt on mine.

How he touched me.

How he felt inside of me.

How he made love to me.

How he made me *feel*.

I convinced myself that the reason for the infatuation—the only explanation I could find—was because he'd been the only man who had truly seen the unabridged version of myself. Both in Vegas, and here.

What I usually hid, or held back from everyone else, he got to see because I was unafraid of his judgment. Usually happens when you're convinced you will never see someone again and give yourself permission to just be you. Of course, when I did see him again, it was too late. Plus there was my anger at my work situation and my stupid idea I was going to sabotage him and run him out of town. I had been so busy concentrating on all of that, I neglected to put up my usual walls. So, I stayed and he got me—the first man ever, maybe even person—uncensored.

Such wonderful revelations.

And much like my failed engagement to my asshole-soon-to-be-felon ex-boyfriend, I'd learned it too late.

So, it was for the best.

That was the lie I told myself as I went to work and saw him every day.

He wouldn't have wanted a relationship; he wouldn't have wanted anything long-term so ultimately he would have broken my heart.

So it was for the best.

Besides, he might go back to Chicago or be promoted here, so it would have all ended eventually. And just because what we were doing was technically not against the rules, I'm sure it would have been frowned upon.

So it was for the best.

God, I hated that phrase.

Even in my head it sounded like utter bullshit.

Well, there was one positive out of all of this mess—we were an amazing team.

Seriously, he was incredible and it was beautiful to watch. He had amazing instincts and was aggressive in just the right way. There were other things too. He had an added insight from his experience at Stockwell which was something I lacked. And I had learned more in the past two months with Kyle by my side than I did in the months after Vegas. He listened, appreciated my input, and we made decisions together.

And as much as I hated to admit it, I hadn't been ready to take on the job by myself. Caleb and Adele had been right, I would have died trying to succeed but I would have crashed and burned epically. He on the other hand probably would have been fine without me but it had been the right choice to pair us together.

As a team, we were unstoppable.

Such a shame I couldn't have it all.

It was for the best.

SHUT THE FUCK UP!

"What did you say?" Kyle stood in the open doorway of my office, confused.

"Nothing, computer frustrations." I pointed to my monitor that thankfully had thirty-five tabs open of Excel spreadsheets. At least that looked convincing even if I didn't.

"I still prefer hardcopies."

He smiled.

That beautiful, wonderful smile that hitched a little higher on the left. "Going between the tabs drives me crazy, and I work better when I can physically have it in my hands."

Yeah, those hands were fantastic so I totally understood.

"I just think of all the trees I'd kill with the printing. It feels wasteful." I sighed, not really giving a shit about the paper, or the trees, or the thirty-five spreadsheets. "But thanks for the tip."

Another smile. "Don't mention it."

It was for the—

"Hey!" An email alert popped up on my screen confirming the cancelation of the two o'clock appointment. "Did you accidentally mess with my schedule?" I hoped I hadn't left it open when I'd been logged onto his computer earlier. "My meeting just cancelled."

The meeting was for Skyline.

Initially it was going to be my vehicle to prove how superior I was to Kyle. I was going to reel in a seven-figure client and ride into Caleb and Adele's office like a conquering emperor, showing what I had accomplished, all by myself. Then they would see how obviously amazing I was and send Kyle packing. Or that had been the plan.

Of course, now I no longer needed to prove myself and certainly didn't want Kyle to leave. We had shown solid growth in marketing sales, but I'd decided to try and close them by myself anyway. For the experience and the distraction. And because I couldn't just let go of something I'd put so much effort into.

"Your meeting with Skyline?" Kyle asked, watching carefully

for my reaction. "The client you didn't tell me about? No I didn't cancel it, but we don't want their business."

So he'd found out about it, and while I hadn't told him, there hadn't been any rules that stated I *had* to share every single client. It was just business, and—yeah, I'll admit it didn't look great—but it still didn't answer the question as to why my two o'clock meeting was history.

It had to be a mistake.

They wouldn't just cancel.

All that time.

The back and forth.

I had been so close to securing the contract.

A chill crept up my spine. A feeling so terrible it shook me to my very core. There was something very wrong.

"What did you do?" I whispered, confused about what was happening and what it meant. "Kyle, why would they cancel the meeting?"

He had to have something to do with it. I wasn't sure how, but deep down in my core, I knew he was responsible.

My throat tightened, a lump forming at the base of it as I tried to blink back tears. The last thing I wanted to do was cry in front of him, but my emotions were already close to bubbling over.

"Sarah." His voice softened as he looked at me. "It's for the best. Trust me, sweethear—" He caught himself, glancing either side before stepping into my office and closing the door. He took a breath, his chest rising and falling as he met my eyes. "They cancelled the meeting with you because they signed with Stockwell an hour ago."

"What?" I leapt out of my seat so fast my chair fell back onto the floor. "Do you know how much time I spent working on this? The hours I invested? How could you do this to me?"

I was furious. We were equals, and sure, I didn't tell him about it, but that's because I had started it before he'd arrived. And while my motivations for landing the account had changed, they were *my* big fish, he didn't get to snatch it away and give it to someone else.

"We do *not* want to get into bed with them, and if you had bothered to tell me about this earlier I could have demonstrated exactly why." It was the first time ever I'd heard him raise his voice. It wasn't quite shouting, but loud enough to make me jump. "We are supposed to be a team."

"A team?" My whole body shook. "Is that what you call it when you sabotage me?" I was so angry, so upset I could barely breathe.

Maybe I had seen this all wrong. Maybe while I had been celebrating how awesome we were he was secretly looking for a way to get even. To show how inept I was so I would go back to where I belonged and he could be the supreme ruler. Or maybe he was punishing me, annoyed I'd stopped being his little plaything, and him being so cool about it had been an act. What I'd mistakenly thought was compassion and kindness were his way to throw me off my game, so he could crush me like I was nothing.

But why the hell would he give them to a competitor? One he conveniently used to work for? As realization dawned on me, my heart sunk even lower, the thought I could have been played to such a huge degree making me want to be physically ill.

God, I'd been an idiot. Believing everything could be so perfect, and there could be no weirdness, and no hard feelings. What a joke. It had been a set up the whole time. He never cared about me, or Baldwin & Blake. Hell, he probably laughed at me, musing how easy I'd been, getting to have sex with me like it was some fringe benefit while he partook in corporate espionage. He was going to take the company down and me along with it.

"Have you been spying for them the whole time?" I felt sick, knowing what I could have possibly been a part of. "Feeding them information?"

"What?" His eyes narrowed as his jaw clenched. "You have no idea what you are talking about." His fists white-knuckled at his sides.

"And what, you found out about Skyline and you just couldn't stand that I could do it without you. That *Stockwell's golden boy who closed his first seven-figure deal in the first three months* wasn't part of the process. Because how dare anyone else succeed. So you ran back to them? It wasn't really back considering you never really left." I looked at the B&B screensaver on my computer monitor, my heart literally breaking.

"Jesus, Sarah. Are you insane?" He moved closer to me. "Are you actually hearing what you are saying right now?"

"How dare you." I struggled not to yell, the words coming out strangled from my throat. "What makes you think you have any right to speak to me like that? To call *me* crazy when the evidence is right there. I know maybe I handled things with us badly—"

Oh God, what if the whole thing wasn't as big of a coincidence as I first thought? I felt like I was going to be sick. "Was I part of it? In Vegas, did you know who I was?"

"Are you fucking kidding me right now?" His usual self-control shattered as he looked at me with complete disbelief and horror. His shoulders rolled with tension, his eyes narrowing as his jaw tightened. "You think this has anything to do with that? Wow,

Sarah. I knew you didn't think very highly of me, but believing I would fuck you, use you and then ruin the company you work for is pretty fucked up."

"Get out." I pointed to the door trying my best not to scream it. "Get away from me."

He didn't move, his face completely unreadable.

"I'll leave," he said slowly, his eyes on me the entire time. "I'm going to say what I'm going to say and then I'm fucking walking out of here. But you are going to hear what I have to say first." He paused, taking a breath. "Skyline uses sweatshops in third-world countries."

"No, I checked." I shook my head. Emotional or not, he wasn't going to try to get out of this with misdirection. "The manufacturing plant is in Mexico and it's—"

"Mexico is a warehouse. They import the goods premade, park them for a while to make it look legitimate and then bring them across the border. So while it looks like that's where they are made, they aren't. The brand that preaches female empowerment? Pays their mostly female workers pennies. They work twelve-hour days in appalling conditions with girls as young as six being recruited."

"What? I checked. I know I checked." He was confusing me, trying to trick his way out of the deceit.

"You did. And on the surface it all looks fine. But apparel, especially sportswear, is notorious for this kind of thing. Skyline isn't publically listed and the reason is so they don't have to disclose that information to shareholders."

"But—"

"Sarah, you left the Skyline file on your desk my first day here. I saw it before we went to the bar." He gave me a sad smile. "I get it.

The hunger, wanting to prove yourself to the boss. Which is why I made some of my own private inquiries. If everything checked out fine, then you would have had your meeting as planned. And I don't doubt you would have closed them better than anyone. But when I found out how shady they were, I couldn't let you go through with it. When they are exposed, they will be ruined. They aren't just unethical; they violate basic human rights. Aligning yourself with a company like that—"

"Career suicide," I choked out.

It hadn't been sabotage—he'd saved me. Even though it had been my mistake and my arrogance for not asking for help, he still had my back. Even after all those horrible things I'd said.

"But why Stockwell?" I still didn't understand the connection.

He took a long, slow breath and then exhaled.

"I left Stockwell Media when Keith Stockwell's son tried to rape my sister."

"What?"

I felt like my legs were going to go out from under me, my fingers grabbing at my desk to help me keep standing.

"Keely was housesitting my place, I was away on business and Carter Stockwell decided to show up. He'd always had a thing for her even though she was married. When Mike got there, Carter had Keely naked, crying and pinned down—"

He stopped and looked at me, his face a mix of emotions I couldn't read. Guilt? Anger? A lump in my throat made it hard to swallow as I watched him tense, needing him to go on but not wanting to ask him to continue.

"I should have been there, it was in my fucking house, god-damn it." He ran his hand roughly through his hair. "Mike took care of it, beat the living shit out of Carter and called the cops."

"Thank God. Is she okay?" My heart was racing, unable to imagine how she must have felt. What *he* must have felt.

It was obvious he felt responsible even though there was no way he could have stopped it. I wanted to reach for him, to reassure him in some way. But I didn't dare, locking my hands at my sides as I watched him pace.

"Things got complicated because the Stockwells have fancy attorneys and Carter almost died after Mike got through with him."

I could feel his anger, his pain—all of it in the way he moved. His body coiled tight, like at any moment something would snap.

"So, they agreed to drop assault charges on Mike if Keely dropped the attempted rape charge on Carter. Of course she does, even though both of us tell her it's a bad fucking idea. So what does Stockwell do the minute his piece of shit son walks free? He offers me a raise and a promotion, shaking my hand, thanking me for my cooperation." He barked out a humorless laugh, his hand clenching into a fist.

"Can you believe that? Obviously I walked, they threatened to ruin me if I talked about it, told me not to be stupid and take the job and the money. And even though I'd earned it, worked my fucking ass off for that man, there wasn't a figure he could write which would be big enough for me to stay. If I stayed I was going to finish what Mike started, maybe take a shot at his old man too. And if we couldn't get them with criminal charges, then I'd get them the one place it would hurt. His wallet and his reputation."

"So that's why you gave them Skyline."

"Stockwell was conveniently *tipped off* that Skyline was shopping around. They had your figures and undercut you like I knew they would. It helped they knew they were beating out a company I now worked for." He gave me a sad smile.

"I figured they belonged together, especially considering the reporter friend of mine who helped me gather all the information was going to run an exposé. He is going to hold off for a couple of days, just to make sure he gets all the facts straight, but when this blows up, Stockwell's share prices are going to tank so badly it's going to take years to recover."

If the whole situation hadn't been so incredibly sad—Kyle's poor sister being subjected to that animal—Kyle's plan of revenge would have been ingenious. He not only exposed a company who was violating and abusing people, but got the people who had done the same to his sister to go down with it. The whole time keeping his hands clean. Everything was legal.

God, I was so so stupid.

How could I have even thought—"Kyle, I don't know what to say."

I wanted to take it back, to stop the way he was looking at me with such hurt. The smile that I loved so much—gone.

"Nothing to be said."

And he turned to walk out the door.

19

I WAS A PLANNER.

When I had facts and figures laid out in front of me, I felt like there was nothing I couldn't accomplish.

I needed assurances.

Even if they were only probabilities, I needed to know there was a chance before I put myself on the line. It's the way I operated, the way I had always been.

But watching Kyle ready to walk out that door threw everything I knew about myself right out the window.

I didn't wait.

I didn't think.

I didn't plan.

Instead I ran, throwing myself in front of the doorway and barring his exit.

Like an escapee from an insane asylum.

"No, don't leave." My head shook, my arms locked across the doorframe. "Please don't leave."

Never in my life had I thrown myself at a man's feet and begged him to stay.

Not even when the man I had dated for two years, and who had committed to marry me, dumped me two days before our wedding.

Never.

But I was begging now, and I would do anything if it meant Kyle didn't walk out the door.

"I'm sorry. I am sorry about everything." My mouth kept talking, desperate to say something that would convince him.

"Sarah, what are you doing?" He took a step closer, his head shaking.

I couldn't tell if he was horrified or embarrassed for me, and the way he was looking at me maybe it was both. But I didn't care. I deserved it—I had been a horrible person. And if I were him I probably wouldn't forgive me, I just hoped—no I *prayed*—he was a better person than I was.

"I was an idiot, okay? I made a huge mistake." *Please let me get the words out.* "I'm not used to people seeing me like you did. I got scared and freaked out. And even if we only dated for a year—or even if it was a month—it would never have been a waste of my time. You are the only person I can be my true self around. Who not only isn't intimidated by me, but actively encourages me to be strong, to push myself out of my comfort zone. I was too scared, too stupid to see it. Please, *please*—give me another chance."

He was disgusted.

I was sure of it.

His brows were knitted tight with his mouth in a thin line as he raked his hand through his hair in frustration.

I couldn't stop.

I *wouldn't* stop.

He shook his head, unconvinced. "Not only did you not trust me, but believed I would betray both you and the company. That I was the type of person who was *capable* of any of that."

He was so close, his body inches from mine, and I knew there was no way I could physically restrain him if he truly wanted to leave.

"Because I didn't trust myself. Because I am the type of person *capable* of that. And I guess it made me feel better about myself hoping I wasn't the only one. Because *I* am that terrible. "

There were so many things I wanted to tell him.

How I'd intended to undermine him, to actively try and sabotage him. How the whole Skyline thing started in an effort to prove I didn't need him. How if it had come to a decision between saving him or myself, I *probably* would have chosen me. And in a way I did when I told him I didn't want to see him anymore.

All the words that would have explained so much, but I just couldn't say.

"I knew I'd fall in love with you," I said instead. "I knew that my heart wouldn't have the choice even though my head thought it was a bad idea. And I was so afraid because I've never been in love before. Not even when I was going to marry someone else. Deep down I knew I wasn't *really* in love, not like I knew I would be with you."

It was like he stopped breathing.

Or maybe I did.

Or maybe we'd entered a vortex where air and time no longer existed.

And I didn't care, if I could just have one more minute with him.

"I would have fallen in love with you too," he said slowly. "And for the record, it wouldn't have been *that* bad of an idea."

It was small.

The tiniest twitch on the corner of his mouth.

But I saw it.

And then he gave me a smile.

His perfect, amazing smile that could thaw an entire ice cap. Or the heart of a complete and utter bitch. Me, in case anyone was wondering.

"I'm sorry. Please. *Please*. If there is anything, *anything* I can say or do—"

He didn't give me the chance to finish.

Instead he kissed me.

His mouth owned mine as he wrapped his arms around me and pulled me away from the doorway, our bodies a mess of limbs.

"I liked it better when you didn't ask for permission." His hands moved down to my ass and hauled me onto his body. "So, stop saying sorry and show me the girl I married in Vegas."

God, that night felt like a lifetime ago.

So much had changed.

"No." I kissed him, taking charge of his lips while my hands knotted into fists at his shirt. "I'd rather show you the woman I am right now."

He gave me another perfect smile as I moved my mouth to his ear. "And you aren't going anywhere."

Epilogue

Sarah~Five months later

"SARAH, TAKE A SEAT."

Caleb Baldwin smiled as he tipped his chin to the chair in front of him.

"You're both here." I nodded to Adele sitting beside him as I lowered myself into the chair. "If you're trying to let me down easy, you don't need to. Whatever decision you've made, I know it will be the right one."

Amazing how much a person could change in a few short months.

And I had learned plenty.

About myself, about the business—and most of all about how to be better at *both* those things.

Kyle Drake—the amazing man who I had the privilege of working with, who also happened to be my boyfriend—had a lot to do with that.

Neither of us knew what Caleb and Adele's intentions were.

Originally we were to share the senior marketing role. It would give me the much-needed experience and support and also help Kyle assimilate to Baldwin & Blake in New York.

While there was no chance of him returning to Chicago, and I had grown in my own right, we always suspected the sharing of our positions would be temporary. And if there was one person who deserved it, who was better and able to do the job with his eyes closed, it was Kyle. And I would happily work by his side. After all, he had not only saved my career, but my reputation as well, with the Skyline fiasco. Unfortunately for Stockwell, they hadn't fared so well. After the story ran, the company ended up being cannibalized, unable to recover from the huge stock drop.

"Your attitude seems to have changed a little since the last time." Caleb smiled, a silent expression passing between him and Adele.

"Yeah well," I laughed remembering back to that day. "I still don't think there is anyone who wants it as much as I do, but I'm not so arrogant to think I know everything just yet. I plan on having a very long and prosperous career with Baldwin & Blake, and I will patiently, with acquired experience, work my way up."

"Sounds like a senior marketing manager to me, what do you think, Caleb?" Adele smiled and then nodded to her husband.

"Yeah, it sure does," he agreed, and slid a piece of paper in front of me.

"The job is yours, Sarah. And Kyle's," he added as I tried to read what was written on the page. "We expanded the position, so between the two of you, you will head your own department. Both you and Kyle proved that not only do you work well together, but as a team have grown our profit margin and brought in new and exciting clients. And that's exactly what we were looking for."

"Oh my God!" I clutched the paper to my chest, my heart pounding so hard I was sure it wasn't healthy. "Both of us?"

"Yes, both of you," Caleb confirmed.

They'd known about our relationship shortly after we'd gotten back together. As Kyle had said, we weren't breaking any rules so other than been given a stern talking to, we didn't suffer any HR nightmares. Not that I absolutely wouldn't have gone through whatever hell I needed to if it meant we got to be together. Even if it had meant leaving Baldwin & Blake, having Kyle—*loving* Kyle— would have been worth it. Thankfully, I'd never needed to make that choice.

"I know it can be hard working with someone you care about." Adele looked lovingly at Caleb and there was no doubt she wasn't talking about Kyle and me. "But we, of all people, know you can have business with a relationship; we made it work and we know you will too," she added.

"Coming from you, that is a huge compliment, thank you." I rose out of my seat and shook both of their hands. "Thanks for everything."

As I closed the door behind me and walked out into the hall, I could only remember one day where I'd ever felt so happy. Co-incidentally, it was also the day where I'd also felt my worst. The day I stopped being afraid and opened my heart to Kyle.

It wasn't easy—we still had some ups and downs—but I wouldn't trade being his girlfriend for anything.

"So what's the verdict?" The man in question was waiting just around the corner. His hands wrapping around my waist as he brought his mouth down on mine.

We tried to keep emotional displays out of the office but every once in a while one or two crept in. Kennedy agreed that I shouldn't fight it and it was really hard working with your hot boyfriend and not kissing him.

"The verdict is I love you, and you are awesome. And I am very happy." I kissed him back unable to contain myself.

It wasn't the first time we'd said I love you, that had happened a couple of months ago. He had been the one to say it first. And then he showed me in a way only Kyle could. He had me screaming his name so much I almost lost my voice and then when we were done, I said it right back. Now that we had said it, it was like we couldn't stop.

"And I love you too." He dropped a soft kiss on my nose. "But, I want to know which one of us is going to be the other's bitch. Should I brush up on my coffee making skills or do I start fantasizing about you calling me sir? Actually, we can try the sir thing at home later. I'm getting hard just thinking about it."

Kyle

I wasn't lying about getting hard.

It was an occupational hazard when I kissed Sarah, especially when she was happy.

Those tight skirts she wore didn't hurt either; they might have been knee-length and respectable but I knew what was underneath.

And as far as the job was concerned, I didn't care either way.

While I loved working at Baldwin & Blake, I'd found something I loved more.

Much more.

So, if that meant stepping aside then that was no problem. There were other jobs, other companies but there was only one

Sarah. And she was mine.

"If I have to call you sir, what will you call me? She bit her lip, seductively.

Great. Now I was even harder.

"I will call you *fucked* if you don't stop that." I wasn't kidding either. While we had managed to make it this far without defiling her office or mine, I could only resist so long. Her smiling, looking at me like that, and it would be worth whatever trouble we attracted. "Can you spell sexual misconduct?"

"You know," she got serious for a minute, "if either of us becomes the other's boss, it invalidates the exemption on the fraternization policy. You worried?"

She was killing me.

If there was a woman who could bring me to my knees, it was the woman I was holding right now.

And what's more, I was enjoying every last excruciating second.

"Nope, not at all. And I'm surprised you are." I moved my mouth back to hers; thankful the hall had remained deserted. "Because if you'd read the *entire* policy, you would have seen there is a loophole where it doesn't matter."

She stopped, confused. "What are you talking about, there's no loophole."

"Section two, paragraph one disagrees." I put my hand in my pocket and pulled out the small velvet box I had bought at lunchtime. "It's not *fraternization* if you're my wife."

"Oh my God." Her hand flew to her mouth as she looked at the ring. "You want me to marry you?"

It was probably a little soon and impulsive since neither of us had really spoken about marriage. But I didn't need to wait any longer to know she was the one for me, and I wasn't giving her a chance to get away a second time. Besides, I *really* liked calling her my wife.

"Yeah, I figured we'd get two tickets to Vegas." I took the ring out of the box and put it where it needed to be. She hadn't said yes, but I was quietly confident she wouldn't say no. I was arrogant like that. "I know a great place, I met my first wife there."

She laughed, staring at the ring on her finger. "Keely would kill us."

"She'd get over it." My concern for my sister's feelings ranked lower than my desire to remarry Sarah. Only this time, it was going to be legal. "So what do you say? You want to plan a wedding? Or do you want to hop on a plane and get married by Fat Elvis again? Just a word of warning, if he looks at your tits like he did that last time, I'm going to knock him out."

"I say let's go to the airport and see when the next plane is to Vegas." She smiled, wrapping her hands around me.

"You sure?" I asked. "This one is binding." Giving her one last chance to change her mind.

"Positive," she answered with no hesitation.

"Great, so now that we have that straightened out." I gave her another kiss for good measure. "Tell me what they said."

"Does it matter?" she asked, her hand flashing her shiny new diamond.

"To me?" I shrugged. "Not a bit."

"Good, then let's get married and we'll talk business later." She smirked and yanked on my shirt.

I pulled her into a hug, kissing her forehead. "I have such a smart wife."

She laughed. "I'm not your wife yet."

"Yes. Yes you are."

THE END

To keep up to date with all T Gephart's news, appearances and releases, please subscribe to her mailing list.

Acknowledgements

AS ALWAYS, THE FIRST THANKS goes to my amazing family Gep, Jenna, Liam and Woodley. You guys continue to be awesome, and I hope I make you as proud as you make me.

Thanks to my extended family and friends, I'd name you all but I'm giving you the gift of plausible deniability. You're welcome.

Thanks to Gayle Williams, my "person" extraordinaire. Look at all the stuff we're learning, so glad to have you on my team. #TeamAwesome #LinksInBio #LordHelpUs

Thanks to the Team Brower—Kimberly, Aimee and Caroline. Love working with you all.

Thanks to Nichole Strauss from Insight Editing for making sure I don't sound like a crazy person when my fingers write words my brain clearly didn't approve. You're like an editorial Robert Langdon, deciphering me like a cryptex.

Thank you to Christine Borgford for making my pages look so pretty. YAY, for doing it again. I adore you.

Thank you Hang Le!!! Don't ever leave me, I can't do stock photo hell without you. Ninja hugs to you and all the amazing covers you have made me including this one!

Thank you to my eagle eye proofreaders Lisa B and Rosa. This one was nice and short.

Special thanks to my author friends and are with me on this

amazing journey. Thanks to the Imperfect World OG crew for making writing this story (initially) so much fun. Love you all, don't be strangers!

A HUGE thank you to all the bloggers, reviewers, bookgramers, group admins and promoters, who read, promote, review, and share my work. No matter how big or small you believe your audience is, that you've chosen to include me, rocks my world. A million thanks.

Thank you Liz, MJ and Jillian at 1001 Dark Nights.

THANK YOU SO MUCH to the T Gephart Review Crew and Entourage. You are my safe place; I love the group and all the crazy that comes with it. Thanks to all the guys who share, comment and like.

Special Thanks to the review crew! Your help with releases is invaluable!!

And thank YOU—the person holding this book, Kindle, iPad, Phone or however it is you're reading this. Without you these are just words on a page. So thanks for picking it up and reading. #TellYourFriends.

About the Author

T GEPHART IS A USA Today and International bestselling author from Melbourne, Australia.

With an approach to life that is somewhat unconventional, she prefers to fly by the seat of her pants rather than adhere to some rigid roadmap. Her lack of "plan" has resulted in a rather interesting and eclectic resume, which reads more like the fiction she writes than an actual employment history. She'd tell you all about it, but the statute of limitations hasn't expired yet. But all those crazy twists and turns have led her to a career she loves—writing romantic comedy.

When she isn't filling pages with sassy and sexy characters with attitude, she's living her own reality show in the 'burbs of Melbourne with her American husband, two teenage children, and her fur child—Woodley.

She loves adventure, to laugh, travel, and strives to live her life to the fullest.

www.tgephart.com

Books by this Author

The Lexi Series

Lexi

A Twist of Fate

Twisted Views: Fate's Companion

A Leap of Faith

A Time for Hope

The Power Station Series

High Strung

Crash Ride

Back Stage

The Black Addiction Series

Slide

Sticks

Stand

#1 Series

#1 Crush

#1 Player

#1 Rival

#1 Lie

#1 Muse

#1 Love

Collision Series

Train Wreck

Car Crash

Standalones

The Fall

One-Night Stand-In

Viral

Send Me Crazy (coming soon)

www.ingramcontent.com/pod-product-compliance
Lightning Source LLC
Chambersburg PA
CBHW030430120726
47903CB00003B/889